THIS IS A UCHRONIAN NOVEL.

The term "uchronian" is a new-old one
. . . it derives from a book published
in the 19th Century about the world as
it might have been had history developed
otherwise. In short, a uchronian novel is
what used to be termed "a world of if."

*But now that science fiction accepts the
possibilities of parallel worlds and an in-
finity of alternate universes, these worlds
may be as real as the one in which we
happen to live.*

ALL TIMES POSSIBLE is a uchronian
novel about America as it could easily
have been had there been some slight
divergencies in the political currents of
the past few decades.

It is the novel of a young idealistic American named Tommy Bloome who realized the possibility of changing history
and set out to remold the world his own
way.

*It may be as relevant as tomorrow night's
speech by the president.*

ALL TIMES POSSIBLE

Gordon Eklund

DAW BOOKS, INC.
DONALD A. WOLLHEIM, PUBLISHER

1301 Avenue of the Americas
New York, N. Y.   10019

FIRST PRINTING, JUNE 1974

1 2 3 4 5 6 7 8 9

PRINTED IN U.S.A.

Prologue

Standing in the middle of the torpid, sweating, languidly milling Fourth of July mob, Timothy O'Mara was unconscionably aware of a single indisputable truth: he was a dead man. At twenty-three and while still retaining all the vigorous powers of moving, breathing, speaking, smiling—but dead. As dead as any ancient moldering carcass in a graveyard. A dead man. He knew this.

O'Mara hated this mob which surrounded him. The bulk of the mass was so tightly compressed around him that he could barely manage to shift his feet often enough to keep the soles from burning up as the blistering heat rose off the pavement and pierced the cracked bottoms of his battered shoes. He had to fight the mob physically to obtain the simple privilege of raising a hand and wiping the sweat from his lips and chin and brow. His shirt lay plastered flat against his shoulders. Even though it was a hot day, he was wearing a heavy winter jacket with a fur collar and thick cotton inner lining. The jacket was the only one he owned. Various segments of the mob, shifting in casual summer shirtsleeves, glanced curiously at his strange dress. Who is this man? they must have wondered. Worker? Student? Bum? O'Mara ignored them. If they wanted to know who he was—well, they'd be finding out soon enough. He grinned and shoved his hands deep in his jacket pockets, feeling the secure chill of hard steel. He laughed aloud. The gun carried eight shots, but he didn't expect the mob to let him get off more than three or four. Then they'd kill him —the mob—merely confirming the acknowledged fact of his end. But I've got to get that son of a bitch first, he thought. When I die, I'm going out as a murderer, the same as the rest of them. He directed his thoughts toward the mob: Hey, you, all of you, turn around and listen. Take a careful look at the man named O'Mara who stands in your midst. See that silly stupid jacket he's wearing? Well, brother, let me tell you—don't laugh, there's a loaded gun in the pocket of that jacket. Take a real close look at that man, brother, for he's the one who's going to set you free.

Set them free? O'Mara shook his head, knowing full well he wasn't setting anyone free but himself.

Kiley came slinking over and pressed his lips to O'Mara's ear. "He's not coming. Damn it, Tommy, I can feel it. He ain't going to show."

"Look," he told Kiley, whispering as softly as possible, "don't even talk. He'll be here."

"But, Tommy—"

"Shut up." He grabbed Kiley by the sleeve. "It's almost time. Let's move up now."

"Good." Kiley nodded sharply. "I know where too. You won't have to worry about me, Tommy."

"I hope not."

The two men separated, then moved forward. O'Mara did not look around. He was satisfied Kiley would accomplish this part all right. It was later, when the guns were out, that he worried about. You better make sure you shoot, you son of a bitch, he thought.

Toward the front of the square, a speaker stood upon a high platform, ranting at the crowd. Senator Fairbanks, California's own. This close O'Mara couldn't help hearing.

"This is the time to remember those men and women who have willingly surrendered their very lives so that this nation and her blessed allies might continue their firm and ceaseless struggle against that vast rising red tide of tyranny which threatens to bury the world beneath her deep red swirling waters, but more than that, worse than that, to consume our very souls, our freedoms and liberties, feeding as a parasite does upon the remains of mighty beasts. I say —and Mr. Rader does too—we all say: let America hear the music of our voices. And more than that: let the whole world, rich and poor, white and black and yellow, free man and slave, let them pause to listen and so hear and thus know that we Americans who stand here today do solemnly vow that we shall not cease in our holiest of missions until the deed has finally been done and the world in its entirety is once again free and whole and equal. Let us tell the world—and proudly—without apology: we are Americans.

"I am not ashamed to say these words. I say them to you now, this fourth day of July. I shout them gloriously: I am an American!"

"I am an American!" shouted Timothy O'Mara, continuing to approach the podium. Everyone was shouting. They were all Americans—each and every one of them: rich and poor, humble and proud, adult and child, white and black and red and yellow.

O'Mara stopped. This was close enough. The mob stood as thick as pudding here. A dozen rows, no more, between him and the platform. A few of the closest heads belonged to soldiers but none seemed to be taking their work excessively seriously. Why worry? This was an American mob. The whole of it. Good, honest, true, loyal Americans. Me too, Timothy O'Mara thought, and he touched his gun.

"I am an American!"

He could see Kiley in position on the other side of the platform. That meant both of them were ready. If not me, O'Mara thought, then him. One of us has to get him.

Fairbanks was talking again. "Now, ladies and gentlemen, we must pause briefly in our ceremonies. The Sixth Army Band from the Presidio of San Francisco has agreed to lead us in a rendition of the national anthem. Afterward, General Davis D. Norton, as promised, will discuss the progress of our Oriental crusade. Following that, Mr. Rader himself will address us over the radio from Washington. For myself, I thank you for the attention you have bestowed upon me this glorious day." He flashed a massive grin, waved his arms briefly but furiously, then disappeared.

Fascist fucking bastard, O'Mara thought, waiting, waiting. The band began to play. O'Mara sang with the rest:

> Oh, say can you see
> By the dawn's early light
> What so proudly we hailed
> At the twilight's last gleaming . . .

He sang boldly, loudly, happily, and why not? O'Mara loved to sing and, being a dead man, was never going to get another chance. As a boy on the small Colorado ranch (farm, actually), the whole family had gathered most nights (especially in winter) and sang with each other. That was way back when, before the start of the war, just after the last upheaval; the singing had ended in '37 when his father had been sent to Manchuria to fight in a war nobody, including him, understood. He had not come back, except that once, *in absentia,* his name at the head of Mr. Rader's telegram: KILLED IN ACTION FEBRUARY 27, 1942, WHILE FIGHTING HIS COUNTRY'S ENEMIES. His country's maybe, but not his own. Kiley knew how he felt. Kiley was here for only one reason: because of his sister. Unlike O'Mara, Kiley made no pretense of giving a damn for the general suffering of mankind. The class struggle was nothing to him but a funny-sounding phrase. But he knew about his sister. He understood how, during the purges, they had taken her torn and shaven body and nailed it to a post in front of City Hall, where the loyal citizens of the city could pass and spit and curse and flay and slice until finally—a week after the ordeal had begun—somebody put a bullet through her forehead one dark night. O'Mara had never known Kiley's sister, Mary, but he had heard she was smart. That couldn't have been true. Smart people did not become dead people except through their own choice. At the time of the final purges in '45, they had chased Timothy O'Mara through half the country and he was still alive this day. After a fashion. Not that his salvation had necessarily been the result of his brains; for the most part—he readily admitted this—it had been simple luck. The luck of a man named Tommy Bloome; O'Mara never denied the debt he owed the dead Bloome. Maybe in heaven or hell or wherever—five or ten minutes from now—he could start paying him back.

A small quiet town in Upper California. Chico, Eureka, Marysville. Coming down a silent street, O'Mara peered furtively through the dirty windows of tiny diners, wishing for the half-dollar necessary to put a full meal under his belt for the first time in a week. He had a dime. Across one empty storefront, posters were tacked like cheap wallpaper. O'Mara recognized four good friends. WANTED—REWARD—DEAD OR ALIVE—TRAITORS. His own face wasn't there, but he had seen it often enough. The photograph they used—the last ever taken of him—had been snapped shortly before his sixteenth birthday. He was hardly the same person now. The first time he had ever seen the poster, dangling from a farmer's picket fence, he had been deeply shocked: that shallow, boyish, sweetly innocent face which had once been his own. The description still largely fit: red hair, green eyes, freckles on cheeks and shoulders. But he was an inch-and-a-half taller and thirty pounds heavier, and the face . . . they'd never catch him on account of the face. He had shivered at the sight; it had been like catching a sudden glimpse of your own ghost.

> Whose broad stripes and bright stars
> Through the perilous night
> O'er the ramparts we watched
> Were so gallantly streaming . . .

Passing another lunch counter, he glanced inside, then stopped suddenly and stood there staring. Seated at the counter, sipping coffee unaware, was the younger face of Timothy O'Mara. It was incredible. Even the size, the build, the freckles.

He went into the diner and sat at the far end of the counter. He ordered coffee, which left him a nickel. Men entered and left. The man behind the counter addressed each familiarly in a thick Swedish accent. Everyone except himself and the other, the man with his younger face. So that meant the man wasn't known here; he was a stranger in town. When the man left the diner, O'Mara followed him out. Streetlamps danced brightly along the edge of the road; here and there a glowing neon sign uttered a silent slogan. A quiet place—people at home, in bed, asleep. O'Mara followed the man to a seedy hotel. After that, he continued down the street, leaving the town behind, and when he found a wide damp ditch beyond the glow of the street-lamps, he crawled into it and slept the night away. The next night, he caught the man with his face near another ditch. His hunting knife rose unceremoniously and slashed down. The man gurgled, spit, gagged, then lay still. Dead. O'Mara calmly switched identity cards. In doing so, he traded much more than a thin piece of sealed cardboard; he traded souls. The man in the ditch, the dead man, became Timothy O'Mara, accused traitor, assassinated by some anonymous patriot. He, in turn, was Tommy Bloome, wandering vagrant. O'Mara was dead; long live Bloome.

> The rockets' red glare
> The bombs bursting in air
> Gave proof through the night
> That our flag was still there . . .

When he reached San Francisco, he had been forced to tell certain people the story behind his new identity. He had shocked them deeply, frightened them. They were paper revolutionaries; murder was an alien act. Kiley frightened them too. He never said "dialectics" or "working class state" or "dictatorship of the proletariat." He had never read a line of Marx and thought Lenin looked funny in that silly beard. Kiley didn't want revolution; he wanted revenge. For a sister shaven and slivered and nailed to a post. The other sisters of other men—the ones in Greenville, S.C., and Butler, Pa., and Jefferson City, Mo.—they meant nothing to Kiley. Only his own blood sister mattered.

Theoretically, the names of the assassins had been picked at random from inside a battered top hat. Before the first name was drawn, O'Mara had known: it would be him and Kiley. Walton said, "Tommy Bloome and"—reaching again into the hat—"Kiley. Jack Kiley."

Kiley failed to protest beyond asking why they didn't place a sharpshooter in a window or a bomb under the platform. "This way me and Tommy don't have a chance of getting away. I don't care for myself, but why waste lives uselessly? If there's another way—"

"Bombs kill the innocent along with the guilty," Walton coldly explained. "And we haven't got a sharpshooter. We haven't even got a rifle, just two handguns. If we want to kill Norton—and we voted we did—this is the only way."

O'Mara hadn't said a word. He knew there was a good and logical reason for picking him: he had killed before. None of the others had ever experienced that moment of true knowledge when a man went squint or squeeze or slice or slash and saw revealed before him the staring eyes of a newly dead man. Once you had lived through that, it was easier the next time. At least he hoped it was easier.

> Oh, say does that star-spangled
> Banner yet wave
> O'er the land of the free
> And the home of the brave.

The mob fluttered expectantly now. O'Mara glanced over at Kiley, failing to catch his eye. But he was there; he had found a good place. It had to work now. They couldn't both miss—could they?—not if both of them fired.

General Davis D. Norton reached the platform. Until recently commander-in-chief of all allied forces on the Asian mainland. He leaned forward on the podium and tilted his head quizzically at the applauding mob. An old soldier. Corncob pipe jutting. A tiny shriveled husk of a man. His uniform hung loosely from his shoulders; his arms were pale white stems protruding from the clipped short sleeves of his shirt.

O'Mara thought, Here is the man I must kill.

General Norton spoke in a halting, quavering, aged voice. He stumbled over certain words and flew quickly past others. "Chinese forces and Soviet troops met forces USA and Japanese Empire upon the field of battle. Stood firm and fast nine days—"

The mob, failing to understand, grew restless. O'Mara touched the comforting presence of the gun. He listened carefully to what the general was saying but made no effort to understand the words. He was waiting to hear a certain phrase. An agent had purloined a copy of the general's approved address. The following words halfway down the fourth page had been underlined in red: ". . . the walls of Shanghai presented an apparently overwhelming obstacle to the advancing allied forces."

O'Mara removed his hand from his pocket and quickly wiped the palm upon his pants. Hurry, he thought. Get your tongue out of your throat. Say it, damn you: *"the walls of Shanghai . . .*

Norton said, "Enemy forces launched a sneak attack. Allies countered properly. Cruiser *Lindbergh* broke river block-ade and proceeded to bombard—"

Hurry, hurry up, thought O'Mara.

Suddenly, quickly, without warning, General Norton said, ". . . walls of Shanghai presented an apparently overwhelm-ing—"

Caught unaware, O'Mara lunged desperately. The gun was out; it shook wildly in the air.

Squint, squeeze, slice, slash.

He fired.

Hearing the shot, O'Mara instantly squeezed again. Wood splintered—the railing around the podium. The general was gone.

Had he been hit? Damn him, damn him, damn him, O'Mara thought. In reading the speech, Norton had skipped a whole long paragraph. Why? Luck? Fate? He couldn't have known.

For the hell of it, O'Mara fired out a third shot.

That was the last.

The mob had reached him now. He had expected them to trample him immediately, but instead they came so slow-ly he was able to pick out certain faces: a young boy, no more than eight or nine; a beautiful teen-aged girl, golden hair and silver teeth; a man dressed in a worn army uni-form, ribbons burning on his chest, left pants leg hollow and flapping. Then they swept over him. He went down, rolling into a ball. The hard pavement struck his face. A wave of flesh smothered him. He lay still, waiting to see if he would survive.

Then he remembered: Kiley.

He hadn't fired. Not a shot. Kiley had turned coward.

Bastard, O'Mara thought calmly to himself. Lousy yel-low chickenshit bastard.

Suddenly, daylight struck his face. He glimpsed a pale youthful face hovering above. A boy in a uniform. A soldier.

"That's the one!" shouted someone in the mob. "Look! He's still got the gun in his hand!"

"Drop it," the soldier ordered calmly. He turned a pistol on O'Mara. "Drop it, then get up."

Obediently, O'Mara released the weapon and staggered to his feet. The mob closed in around him.

The soldier's voice, still calm and controlled: "Get back —move along. Let him up. Clear out of here." The soldier pointed toward the platform. "You go that way."

O'Mara nodded. On the way, he asked, "I missed him, didn't I?"

"Yes, you did."

"I knew I had. If I'd got him, you'd have blown my head off back there. You'd have shown my blood to the mob. As it is, you can kill me anytime."

"I don't know about that," the soldier said.

O'Mara made an effort to keep his backbone stiff; he wanted to hold his head high. The crowd parted obediently to let him pass. They reached a flight of stairs. The soldier pointed. "Up there."

O'Mara mounted the platform. A tall colonel followed with the first soldier.

General Norton was sitting calmly on the wooden floor. Another man—apparently a doctor—hovered over him. As soon as he saw O'Mara, the general struggled to his feet and waved the doctor aside. "So you're the one."

"I am," O'Mara said.

"Then I want you to look at me. Come here—come close —don't be afraid." The general smiled. "I want you to see that you missed me. A little chunk of wood—that was all— it hit me here"—he pointed at his forehead, a narrow ribbon of blood—"but that was all, son. You need pistol practice."

"The next man will be better," O'Mara said. "He won't miss."

"The next man? Oh, come on. Balls to that. There won't be any next man because, after this, we have a perfect excuse for wiping all you red bastards off the face of the earth. Tell me your name."

O'Mara shook his head.

"Trying to act brave, huh? That's a lot of crap. If you had any real guts, you wouldn't have shot at me from a crowd. We'll find out what your name is. I just like to know the people I kill. Sergeant"—he clapped his hands—"pass me your weapon, please."

O'Mara looked at his shoes. He didn't want to watch this part. No, he didn't want to see a damn thing at all.

"You want to tell me why you did it?" Norton asked. "Or do you know?"

O'Mara looked up, seeing the gun as huge as a cannon. "I know. But you'd never understand."

"Balls. But I will tell you something I do understand. I understand killing." His voice was strong, powerful, a far cry from the fumbling tones that had bored the mob. "And I'm going to kill you."

"Liberty," O'Mara said. "Democracy. To make people free. Now do you understand?"

"I understand that you're talking horsecrap." Norton laughed shrilly. "You were going to get all that by killing me? Horsecrap. I know the truth: what you want is to throw us out and take over instead." He paused to gather his strength for a final assault, but "I've been to Russia" was the best he could manage.

"This isn't Russia," O'Mara said, mechanically.

But Norton wasn't listening. "Go fetch Durgas," he ordered. "He'll like to see this."

O'Mara silently studied the gun. A dark shadow fell over him. A tall, thin, hollow-faced man approached. Two enlisted men stepped forward and took O'Mara's arms in theirs. It was only seconds now.

O'Mara stared straight ahead.

Suddenly, at the center of the dark pit of the gun barrel, a tiny red fire glowed brightly. Slowly, steadily, the fire expanded; it spread. There was a noise like the pop of a tiny firecracker. O'Mara shut his eyes, waiting for the pain.

It never came.

Instead, without warning, night fell. One moment it was the middle of the day and the next it was midnight. He looked at the sky and saw that it was blank—no stars, no moon.

Maybe I'm dead, he thought.

But, the next moment, when the sun abruptly exploded in the center of a blue sky, he knew this was not so. He felt the wind, smelled the freshness of the air, heard the distant cry of a bird. Then he heard traffic; a bell clanged.

He wasn't dead.

Opening his eyes wide and swiveling his neck, he saw where he was. Union Square. Midday. Nearly empty. He wasn't dead. But then, in that case, what was he?

Chapter One

He was dead.

That much was clearly established; no doubt could remain. No pulse, no heartbeat, no respiration. Dead. And there was not a thing Doctor Milligan could do to change that irrevocable fact.

He forced himself to move away from the bed. He stood erect. His hands shook; his knees were as weak as water. He needed a drink and had a half-pint flask of bourbon in his bag, but if they smelled liquor on his breath that could only make it worse. They couldn't—he kept telling himself —they couldn't blame him. In fact, he was sure the man was dead before he ever reached the house. But could he prove that? No, no, no, he could not.

He approached the bed again, stepping softly, sliding his feet, afraid of creaking floorboards. He took the ends of the bedcovers between his fingers and drew them back and up so that they covered the white dead face of the man. Only the bright thatch of unkempt orange hair lay exposed to the light. The doctor left that alone.

Now he was actually dead.

Even Doctor Milligan found that hard to accept. He hadn't been old—barely fifty. Nobody had expected him to die. And I was the last one to see him alive, Doctor Milligan recalled. Me. But, no, that wasn't right. It wasn't true. He was already dead when I got here. He had to remember that.

Right now what he really needed, even more than the drink, was fresh air. He had not been out of this room since arriving more than an hour ago and the door had opened only once, when Second Director Lowrey had peeked in and asked if there was anything he could do.

"Get you something to eat, Doctor. Maybe a drink."

17

"Oh, no, sir," Milligan had said. "But thank you."

He pointed at the bed. "He's dead, ain't he?"

"I—I don't know that yet, sir."

"Whenever you do manage to figure it out, don't neglect to let me know."

"Yes, sir. Of course I will. Sir."

Well, now he knew and he hadn't told anyone and the reason was quite simple: he was afraid. He had absolutely no intention of leaving this room until somebody came and got him and made him go.

Aren't they suspicious by now? he wondered, glancing toward the hardwood door. He thought he heard a noise out there and held his breath, but the moment passed—and another—and nothing happened.

Such a hot day too. The Fourth of July. He went to the window and stood there, watching the gentle afternoon breeze sweeping through the stiff branches of the Douglas firs. He hadn't thought of that. What an appropriate day for Tommy Bloome to die. Hadn't Washington or Lincoln or one of those—hadn't he died on the Fourth of July too? (No—he remembered now—it was Thomas Jefferson.)

Tomorrow perhaps, possibly even tonight, his own name would grace the front pages of the world's newspapers. And the radio too. Interviews. But did he want that? Did he dare? What if he fumbled and said the wrong thing? What if they found out about Edward? What if they already knew? Could he possibly trust his own tongue?

"Doctor Milligan, please tell us: what is your frank opinion of the free democracy established by Tommy Bloome in this country?"

"Well, frankly, I loathe it. Free democracy, if you can call it that without laughing, has managed to murder several million people. Including my own brother. I have a private practice. I hate it."

Or—and this thought struck him suddenly—what if they decided there was too much danger in letting him live? What if, as soon as he left this room, they took him away in one of their limousines. The coast was a short drive from here. A deserted road overlooking the surf. The ocean would bury every last trace of his existence.

If only they had told him when they called. He could

have concocted some excuse. He wasn't the only private physician in the area. A stomachache. Car broke down. No gas. Very sorry. Hate to miss the honor but . . .

But the call had not been any different from a normal midmorning emergency. A calm voice. Said it was urgent. Cabin in the woods. Not hard to find. And, Doctor, perhaps you had better come quickly, I think he may be dead.

He had come at once. No hesitation. The door had opened and there had stood the second director. And in the bedroom an even more dreadful sight: Tommy Bloome himself, Tommy Bloome, dead.

What was that?

Doctor Milligan whirled away from the window. A footstep? In the hallway? Silently, he tiptoed to the door and laid an ear close to the wood. He thought he heard it again. There was someone out there. Who?

Standing motionlessly, barely breathing, ear tight against the wood, he strained to hear.

At last he drew away. Now he was crying. He knew it would be awful if they came in and found him this way, but he couldn't stop himself. Tears ran freely down his face. Tears of—what?—rage, anger, frustration, fear. For years he had been wanting to have a cry like this. His body trembled. He clenched his fists. And still he cried.

Finally, he was done. He wiped his eyes and face against his sleeve and went over to the window. He wanted to watch the trees. The sight relaxed him. He saw a small woodpecker rapping at the base of one tree. He felt better now. At least he thought he did. Then, suddenly, he realized with a start that he was crying again.

"Oh, goddamn," he whispered, choking off the words with a fist. "Oh, goddamn it all to hell."

In the main living room of the cabin they sat in opposite chairs with the small couch standing perpendicular between them. The woman was seated so that, when she wasn't talking to the man, her eyes rested upon a set of homemade bookshelves. She knew what kind of books he kept without having to read the titles: biographies of famous historical figures, some straight histories, volumes of communist and socialist theory, and fiction—a fair amount of fiction, none of it any good. The books brought him too near to life for her. And that wasn't right, considering that at this very moment he lay in the first bedroom down the hall either dying or else already dead.

Turning her head away from the books, she faced the man. "Are you sure he's dead?"

"You already asked me that," said Arnold Lowrey.

"Well, tell me again. Tell me the truth."

"O.K., then," said Lowrey. "Here is the truth: nope, I ain't sure if he's dead or not. But if he ain't, if he's alive, then I'll be a mite surprised because it'll mean that Tommy, like Christ, ain't partial to simple death like the rest of us." He smiled at the woman and was disappointed when she failed to respond. Of course, there was a reason for that: she hated him. But it was hard for him to hate her back. She dressed so splendidly—the current ankle-length fashions—and her hair was always neat and natural. He was sure she was the most beautiful woman in the world. He had thought that the first time he had ever seen her—years ago—in 1935, it must have been. Her name was Rachel Bloome.

Lowrey himself was a sloppy man, large but not fat. His nose was a red rubber ball and his eyes tiny peepholes in a fleshy wrinkled face. He was not tall—an inch shorter than Rachel, in fact—and his hair was black, thick, and uncombed.

"You know, Rachel," he said into the silence. "You and me haven't been close like this in a hell of a long time."

"And we won't be again, Arnold. Not ever."

"You got a lot of nerve talking to me in that tone." He laughed suddenly. "Can't you get it straight, Rachel? He ain't here to protect you anymore. Tommy Bloome is a dead man."

"Are you threatening me?"

He shrugged. "Course not."

"Well, you better not. Because I don't give a damn. You can kill me if you want. I don't care." She glanced down the corridor. "Where is that doctor? What's taking him so long."

"Scared," said Lowrey. He lit a Lucky Strike and puffed energetically, spitting tobacco. "He's back in that room with poor dead Tommy and he's shaking in his boots. I had him checked out. His brother belonged to the Freedom League back in the thirties. We hanged him in forty. The doctor's scared I'll say he murdered Tommy on account of the brother. When he gets a firm hold on his guts, then we'll see him."

"You know, you really are a bastard, Arnold. Don't you ever get sick of knowing so many dirty secrets?"

"Oh, I love them." He stroked his jaw, emulating the act of thought. "I know plenty of yours. I could name you every lover you've had since 1940 except"—lifting both hands, he held up the fingers—"like you can see, I haven't got near enough fingers for the purpose."

Rachel deliberately ignored him. Letting her gaze wander, she read the titles of a row of books: *Gone with the Wind; Arrowsmith; So Big; The Magnificent Ambersons; The Green Hat; Laughing Boy; The Thin Man; The Bridge at San Luis Rey.* She broke off here, shaking her head. How long had he had these? How many had he actually read? Not a single one, she bet. Maybe he had meant to—someday—when there was time. And now he was dead.

Lowrey, concealed inside a thick cloud of gray smoke, studied the woman across from him. He was recollecting how, at home in his private library, there was a short film showing this same woman and a man named Carstairs Kennedy engaged in the act of physical love. He smiled at the remembrance and sought to picture himself occupying the position so recently vacated by the late Mr. Kennedy. But he could not do it. No, not Rachel. Every man needed one woman who represented the unattainable ideal in his existence. For most, it was Mother; for Lowrey, it was Rachel. He could no more screw her than he could a goddess. He had his whores and virgins and Negroes and collegians. He had every conceivable variety of woman a man might wish to possess except Rachel Bloome and that was the way it would have to stay.

"Oh, go get him," she said. "Make him come out. I can't stand this anymore. I have to know."

"And scare holy hell out of him? I can't do that. Give the man his own good time."

"That's easy enough for you to say. But I'm tired. How long has it been?"

"Only an hour," Lowrey said.

"It seems like forever."

But now, as if in answer, they heard him coming. The bedroom door creaked and groaned. Footsteps sounded in the corridor. Someone coughed.

"There he is," Lowrey whispered.

"Yes."

Doctor Milligan emerged from the darkness of the hall. His face was white with fear but his step was quick and firm and solid. He ignored Rachel and came straight toward Lowrey.

"Well?" said Lowrey when the doctor reached him.

"Director Bloome, sir. He—he's dead."

"Are you sure of that?" Lowrey said, sharply.

"Yes, sir."

"And when did this happen?"

"About . . . ten minutes ago, sir."

"Well," said Lowrey, standing quickly, "that's just fine." He dropped a friendly arm around the doctor's shoulders and steered him toward the door. Passing Rachel, he winked, saying to the doctor, "You've done a remarkable job. A really fine job. I want you to know I plan to mention your name to the press."

"Oh, sir, that really isn't necessary."

"Sure, it is. We want the whole world to know the kind of dedicated men we have working for this country, even in small towns and rural communities such as this."

"But, sir, I'm still in private practice."

Lowrey winked and hugged the doctor tighter. "We don't have to tell them that, do we?"

"No, sir," the doctor agreed.

The door opened directly off the living room. Lowrey assisted the doctor outside, then paused suddenly and gripped his sleeve. "Say, there is one other thing."

"Yes, sir."

"Your brother. Did you tell me you had a brother?"

"I did have one, sir." He was almost whispering. "But he—he died."

"I'm sorry to hear that. Damn sorry."

"Thank you, sir."

"But maybe I'll be seeing you again soon."

"I—I—"

"Bye," said Lowrey, and he shut the door quickly. Turning back into the room, he looked at Rachel and grinned.

"You bastard," she said.

He sat down and crossed his legs, fingering another cigarette. "Forget that. You heard what the doctor said. Your husband has gone to the next world. But our business is still in this one. I'm going out to the car and call Washington. I'm going to have Tinker rough out a statement. I don't want word of this getting out till I know exactly how to handle it."

"Then you shouldn't have let the doctor go. He'll blab everything."

"Him?" He snorted with disgust. "He won't say a damn word. He won't do a thing that might remind me that he exists."

"And me?" she said. "Surely you haven't neglected me."

"I'll want you at the funeral. That goes without saying. What's today?"

"Friday."

"Say Tuesday, then. Tuesday in Washington. We'll bury him there too. Make a shrine out of it. Raise taxes and build a monument. Do something with this place too. Can't use his birthplace because nobody knows where it is." He turned and looked at the door. "Shouldn't Ennis be coming back pretty soon?"

"He said he was going hunting."

"Hunting? Today? Around here? Why, there's nothing to hunt around here. That son of a bitch! He must've skipped out. He must've known all along it was over while the rest of us kept waiting for the doctor to get off the pot." He shook his head, half admiration, half anger. "But I'll catch up with him. I'll bet you on that."

"I've never doubted your abilities, Arnold."

"Good girl." He stood. "But I've got to get moving. I'm calling Tinker. You stay here." He headed toward the door.

"What are you going to want from me, Arnold," she called after him.

"I'll have a statement written up."

"Will you want me to cry?"

"Hell, yes." His eyes twinkled with merriment. "You give them all you got, which I bet is plenty."

"Thank you, Arnold."

"You bet."

When she was alone, Rachel gave a deep sigh, shut her eyes, and rubbed the sockets tenderly with her knuckles. Tommy—poor Tommy—all the way dead. Did she mourn? Grieve? Did she, in fact, give a damn? For fifteen years and more Tommy Bloome had made up the whole of her life. Her husband, yes, but much more than that. Even after their separation, it hadn't changed: Tommy Bloome was her identity. She wasn't some woman known as Rachel Bloome; she was Rachel, Tommy's wife. And now he was dead and it was like being naked in the middle of a crowd, like having your name stolen away and buried. Who was she now? Rachel Bloome? Tommy's wife? Or was she simply plain old Rachel Malone again? And who was Rachel Malone? Where had she been all these years? What was she now?

Getting to her feet, Rachel (Malone?) (Bloome?) smoothed her skirt across her calves. To the bedroom. Her high heels clicked as she swept briskly past the fireplace, a stuffed salmon mounted over the mantel. She went down the hallway.

The door was open.

The doctor had neglected to close it.

Like a marching soldier, gazing straight ahead, she entered the room. The first thing she saw was the bed. On top, a form covered by a white sheet. Tommy? She saw the hair —bright, orange, fierce—and she stopped.

Why, it is you, she thought. Oh, Tommy—poor dead Tommy.

She pulled the sheet away from his face. She looked. Then lower, exposing his chest, abdomen, groin. She left the sheet bunched at his waist and reached into the stylish thicket of her hair and removed a long straight hairpin.

"Tommy," she said aloud.

She pushed the pin toward his heart. The point easily pierced the pale skin, thrusting down, and then it hit something—a rib?—and stopped.

Hastily, she drew the pin out and peered down at the

wound. Now which was it supposed to be? Blood or no blood?

She couldn't remember.

But he is dead, she insisted. Didn't Lowrey say so? And the doctor? Ennis had known too. Dead, dead, dead.

She turned her back on the dead man. Her eyes were dry. She wouldn't give him—dead or not—the satisfaction. For the radio, the papers, she'd cry for them. But not for Tommy —no, sir—not a single drop for him.

Then she realized that her eyes were no longer dry; she was crying.

"Bastard!" she screamed, turning. "Goddamn dead bastard! When? Tell me when! When are you ever going to leave me alone?"

Chapter Two

In the tiny ugly room the radio played too loudly, abrasive clouds of static rising in sharp contrast to the aura of stark silent grief.

Nadine sat alone, head in hands, and the hands trembled with the pain of sudden loss. Sunlight penetrated an open window. The radio blared and blared. The couch, where she sat, had a broken leg. The chair across from her had a big hole through which a tensed spring could be seen. In the kitchen, a pot of potato soup lay forgotten upon the cold stove. At her feet the morning *Examiner* lay in scattered remnants. Nadine had searched and searched the pages for some clue that might have prophesied the end. Nothing.

SECRET SOVIET PROJECT RUMORED

HITLER AND MINISTERS TOUR LONDON

LETTUCE DROPPED FROM RATION LIST

FELLER SHUTS OUT TIGERS 3-0

LOWREY SEES FURTHER WEALTH SHARING IN '48

But not a word of Tommy Bloome.

When was the last time? Three months ago, maybe four. Africa. She remembered seeing a newsreel segment about Tommy fighting the Germans over there. But nothing, nothing she could remember, not a word since then.

An hour ago. She was moving slowly in the kitchen, heat-ing yesterday's soup. The radio played soft ballads; half-consciously she hummed along.

Then a special announcement: "Please stand by."

So what? Irritated. She switched the dial to another station but the announcement was the same.

A deep, very official voice: "Word has just been received that Tommy Bloome, First Director of the Free Democracy of the United States of America, Chairman of the American Free Democratic Party, died this morning at his vacation home near Neah Bay, Washington. According to official reports, Director Bloome suffered a massive cerebral stroke at an early hour of the morning. In spite of the intensive and dedicated efforts of a team of physicians, he passed away at 1:47 P.M., Pacific Daylight Time. Until this sudden and unexpected attack, Director Bloome had been reported in the best of health and planning an early return to German East Africa, where his work among the revolutionary cadres active there has earned him international acclaim as a friend to the friendless. We now take you direct to Washington, D.C., where the Second Director, Mr. Arnold Lowrey, is about to issue a statement concerning the sudden death of his nearest friend and dearest comrade."

Nadine hadn't listened to that part; she had heard Lowrey before. But she had listened to the next part, and now, as she wept once again, she seemed to hear it once more. "I— I can't believe he's really . . . gone. For the good of my country, I'd rather a million, million others had died, including myself, than Tommy . . ."

That was her—the wife—Rachel. Three years ago during a Democracy Day parade in the city, Nadine had actually seen Rachel Bloome in the flesh. A beautiful woman—fragile, unearthly. Nadine had waved at the passing car and Rachel, turning, had waved back. Nadine had always wondered: did she know me? Had Tommy told her about us?

Suddenly the front door opened.

"Damn it, Nadine, what—"

Sam. He glared at her. His face was dirty; his shirt was soaking wet. He hadn't shaved this morning.

"Tommy Bloome is dead," she told him.

He came into the room with her. "I know that. Why do you think I'm home now?" He smiled. "Tomorrow might be a holiday too." He laughed at her. "Hey, you don't have to cry."

"But on the radio—"

"They told you to cry?" Sam chuckled dryly. "Look, they can't make you do that. They can't catch you if you don't."

"But I want to."

"Ah, come on, Nadine, don't be so dumb."

"I knew him. I'm crying because I knew him." The words slipped out. Sam didn't know about her and Tommy. But did it matter now?

Sam backed off a step and stood regarding her as if he had not seen her before. "You're lying."

"No—no, I'm not."

"You never knew him."

"I did."

"You never had a chance. When was it? You can't tell me."

"Before I met you. Way back. I was only a kid. In 1924."

"Tommy Bloome?"

"He worked for my father."

"Well"—he laughed bitterly—"if you knew Bloome, he sure forgot you. Look at this dump. And my job on the line everyday. He never did much for you."

"I never asked him to."

He gave her a suspicious look. "When did you see him?"

"Never."

"Then you're lying."

"I am not. Don't you remember? Three years ago at the parade. How Rachel waved at me. You said so yourself. She wasn't waving at you or the others—just at me. Tommy must've told her."

"Told her what?"

"About us. About how"—now that the truth was out she couldn't help telling everything—"we were lovers."

"No!" He backed off, fear in his eyes.

"It's true," she said.

He rushed forward and grabbed her wrist. He dragged her to her feet and threw back his fist to strike. But then fear returned to his eyes and he released her and she fell, hitting the couch, rebounding, sprawling on the floor.

"Now look, I'm sorry," he said, speaking in panic. "I didn't mean to . . . you shouldn't have—"

"Shouldn't have what? Shouldn't have told you?" She sat up and smoothed her housecoat down. "You're right too. Because now you've gone and put dirt all over my memories. I loved Tommy and he loved me and you can't ever take that away. You're scared, aren't you? Scared he'll come here and have you killed. Well, don't. Didn't you hear, Sam? Tommy's dead. He's not going to hurt you. You don't have to be scared."

"Lay off," Sam said. "I told you I was sorry."

"Oh, just go to hell." She was crying. "Just go straight there and leave me alone."

And then she was up. Bare feet. Tattered housecoat. She swept past him, darting like a dancer when he reached to stop her, out the door, down the dark hall, toward the stairs. Then up the stairs—one flight, two, three—heart pounding, still running. At the top. Through the heavy door. The roof. Freedom. She stopped, breathing hard, and suddenly laughed.

Oh, Christ, but she wished Tommy was here now. He could hold her in his hands, lay her down, screw her, anything, she didn't care, just as long as he was here.

She crossed the roof, ducking underneath the clean sheets of Mrs. Brown, the underwear of Mr. and Mrs. Leonard, the shirts and skirts and blouses and trousers of the entire Kelly family. Somewhere in the middle of this flapping forest of cloth, she sat down.

It wasn't comfortable here. The roof was covered with loose gravel. It hurt her legs and rear. But she was determined not to budge till Sam came and got her. Maybe he wouldn't come. He always had before, but this time he was scared and that was something different. One time, in the rain, she had waited five hours before he came to bring her down.

She wasn't pretty anymore. The way it was going she'd be fat pretty soon too. No wonder Sam didn't like her so much anymore. Not even forty and already old. Raw red hands, legs with the veins showing, breasts droopy. It was hard being beautiful when you were too poor to care. It was easier to cry. Poor dead Tommy. But she wasn't crying anymore. Up here, the radio below, his death seemed faraway and less real. She wanted to cry. Maybe if she could remember exactly how it had been, then she could cry.

She remembered how, the first time he came to the door, he had looked worse than a scarecrow. That was 1924, so she was sixteen. The ranch lay a mile or more off the main road, so Tommy had walked at least that far. Father, seeing him coming toward the house, turned and said, "We've got a hobo coming here."

But Tommy asked for work.

"Well, now," Father said, guarding the doorway with his great bulk. Behind him, Nadine stood on her tiptoes, catching a vague glimpse of bright orange hair, a pale face, dirty city shoes. "You think you can handle it?"

"Most anything."

"How about milking a cow?"

"I've done it."

"Horses."

"Yeah."

"Clean stables, sweep barns, shovel manure."

"Sure."

"Well, that's a start." Father stepped away from the door and Tommy passed through. Nadine, seeing the whole of him for the first time, thought: he looks awful. Great big holes, like white polka dots, ran up and down both trouser legs and in the rear too, she saw when he walked quickly into the room. He smelled bad—dust and dirt and sweat. It was a hot day in March 1924. Father steered him toward the couch. Mother brought a glass of water.

"Where you worked before?" Father asked.

"Not around here."

"I said where."

"Kansas, Iowa, Nebraska. I was up around North Dakota awhile."

"Born there?"

"Chicago."

"Well, California's different. Farms here aren't family enterprises. It's a business, an industry."

"I know that."

"Harvest time, there's a thousand men in this valley. Sometimes more. Hindus, Japs, Chinamen, some niggers from down South. Not many white men since the end of the war. You don't want to do that."

"I can pick if I have to. But they told me this was a small spread."

"It is. I've got a few acres of apples, that's all."

"I'll work for room and board."

"I can't pay much."

"Room and board and a few dollars for clothes."

"Ten a week."

"You're on."

"Then I'll make you work like the devil. Next month, same as the big growers, I have to harvest. I'll take maybe ten, twelve men to do it. You'll have to run this place and keep an eye on things while I'm watching the pickers."

"I can do that."

"You'll sleep in the barn. A room up in the loft. Got a bed and everything."

"I'll find it." He started to his feet.

"Supper's at six-thirty," Father said.

"You'll see me then." He went on out. Nadine followed and watched through the window, seeing him carry a tiny suitcase across the yard to the barn. From the way he held it, she guessed there was little inside—probably nothing more than a toothbrush, a change of clothes, maybe a razor.

Sharply at six-thirty, Tommy returned. He'd washed his face and shaved, using the cold pump water. He joined the three of them at the table.

"Where you come from?" Father asked. "The city?"

"No, sir. Stockton."

"What were you doing there?"

"Waiting out the winter. I washed dishes in a little diner."

"I'm Ben Kincaid. This is Mary, my wife, and Nadine."

"I'm Tommy Bloome."

Further questions followed. From his answers, it would have been possible to construct an entire life history for Tommy Bloome. It wasn't until years, years later that Nadine discovered nearly everything he'd told them was untrue.

The next day she saw him far out in the fields, a white speck standing clear against the vastness of the morning. She rode closer and saw that he was pitching hay into the back of a horse-drawn wagon. She stopped, jumped down, and stood watching him. Occasionally, she asked him a question, the same ones her father had asked the night before.

Tommy threw the pitchfork, making it stick like a pronged sword in the soft earth. He leaned easily on the handle and squinted against the harsh sun. "I hope it ain't in the air. I hope it ain't catching."

"What?"

"These questions. I think your whole family's got it. An epidemic. Maybe I better just write the whole thing down and let you pass the pages around the supper table."

But then he smiled at her.

Cautiously, Nadine smiled back.

"No hurt feelings?" he asked.

She shook her head. Then she tried to explain why she had asked so many questions and how she was sorry. All the while, Tommy kept smiling. She thought he had the most perfect set of teeth she'd ever seen.

When she finished, Tommy went back to work and this time it was he who asked the questions. Friendly questions, neither intimate nor prying, and she didn't mind in the least answering. He asked about schools and friends and movies. She didn't like school. She had a lot of friends. Charlie Chaplin was funny and Valentino as beautiful as a prince. Her favorite movie was *Way Down East*.

Then he asked about her father. How did he get along with the big growers? What was this association he'd heard about?

Nadine told him everything.

It was right then she first thought she might really be falling in love with him. The rest of that month, she was his shadow. Up at dawn, then down to the barn to watch him milk the cows. Then into the fields, pitching hay, feeding livestock, mending fence. She spent each morning with him and did not leave for school until the last possible moment, hating that place now more than ever. Finally, twelve o'clock and dinnertime, when she'd see him for barely half an hour, ten minutes each way between school, even with digging her heels brutally into Katy's sides, making the old mare gallop like a demon. Saturdays were the best. Tommy worked hard all day and she never once left his side, except when Mother called with kitchen chores, which Nadine performed with tight silent lips until Mother realized it was hopeless and sent her back to Tommy. But anything was better than those terrible wasted classroom hours with Mrs. Perkins discussing the conjugating of verbs and the voyaging of Columbus and the capital of Ohio and what was the square root of the cubed product of two x's and nine y's—she hardly heard a word of any of this. Sunday. That wasn't nearly so good as Saturday. The family went to church and by the time they got back Tommy was usually gone and sometimes he didn't get back till very late at night. Father said, "I'm his employer, not his minister, and where he goes in his free time is none of my business." She didn't understand till later what her father meant, how he thought Tommy went into town and visited the big white house where all the painted women sat in the big front window and Mother always told her to go around that place when she went into that part of town.

But Tommy never went there.

One Sunday near the first of April they came home from church and there wasn't a note from Tommy. She knew that meant he was probably still in his room in the loft. She waited for Father to disappear into the living room to read his paper and Mother was somewhere else, so she slipped out the door and ran across the yard and into the barn. If anyone came, she could always say she had come to get Katy to go riding, but she didn't go near the stables; she went straight up the ladder and rapped lightly on Tommy's door.

"Nadine?"

"Can I talk to you for a minute?"

"It's not locked."

Tommy had fixed up the room very nicely. It even smelled clean, almost sweet. A small window was open. On the bed Tommy lay on his back, head propped against the wall. An open book rested upon a small table Tommy had made by nailing a sheet of plywood across the top of a nail barrel.

"I didn't know you read books," she said.

"Does you father know you're here?"

"I—" She shook her head, but quickly added, "Mother does."

"Oh, yeah?" He didn't say anything else for a long time. Nadine felt embarrassed and would have left if there had been a way of getting out that wasn't worse than staying.

"Did you buy that book?" she finally said.

"Uh-huh."

"How come?"

"I wanted to read it."

"Is it any good?" She came over hesitantly, one step at a time, and peered at the dark letters printed upon the worn spine of the book. She said, "*Theory of the Leisure Class* by Thorstein Veblen." She shook her head, then laughed. "Is that what you want to be, Tommy? Part of the leisure class?"

"Don't you?"

"If it means a millionaire, yes. I'd like to be that."

"Even if it meant robbing people like me?"

"Robbing? Who?"

"Ford, Rockefeller, Mellon, all of them."

"I didn't know they did that. I mean, at first they had to work very hard. Does your book say they're robbers?"

"Not exactly. But they are; all employers rob."

"My father is an employer," she said. "Does he rob?"

"Yes. Him and the growers' association."

"He doesn't belong to them."

"Has he ever tried to stop them?" His eyes were fiercely burning. She had never seen him so intense, waiting expectantly, leaning far forward, hands clenched upon the tabletop.

"Why should he?" she said defiantly.

"To stop them from robbing. The growers don't do the work—the men do, the pickers. Taking a profit from another man's labor is the same as stealing from him."

"Does the book say that?"

"I say that. Don't you think it's true?"

"I . . . no. The land belongs to the growers. They have a right to make a living too."

"Maybe they do," Tommy said, slowly. Suddenly, he smiled, eyes as clear and relaxed as the sky. "But you didn't come out here to talk about that. What is it you want, Nadine?"

"I . . . I . . ." It had been easier before.

"Well, say it. Don't be afraid of me now."

"I wanted to know if you wanted to go riding with me."

"I'd love to, but"—he shook his head—"I don't think I should."

"Are you afraid?"

"No, but I work for him."

"What does that have to do with it? You're still a person."

"I am. But it does mean he can fire me, and I don't want that."

"You are afraid of him." The intensity of her anger amazed her. "He says you go to the whores every Sunday."

Tommy laughed. "This is Sunday. I'm here."

"I . . . I . . ." He wouldn't stop laughing. Suddenly she realized there were real tears in her eyes. That seemed to be enough incentive; she was able to say what she had intended all along: "I love you, Tommy. Oh, I do, I do."

She stayed only long enough to see that he stopped laughing and then she was out the door. Well, she did—she did love him, and she couldn't help it. Down the ladder. Across the floor of the barn. To the rear stall where Katy was kept. She saddled the mare. Tommy, Tommy, Tommy. She would go on loving him forever. He could laugh in her face, do whatever he wanted. Her love for him would never diminish.

She took Katy from the barn and rode that afternoon through rolling green meadows—or so it seemed—not returning until well past dinnertime. Tommy wasn't there; he had eaten and gone back to the barn. Father took her aside and scolded her, saying that if she ever did that again—missing dinner without telling anyone, and Sunday dinner too— why, he'd whip her for sure. "I almost sent Tommy out looking for you. Ten more minutes and I would have."

She told him she was sorry. What else could she say? She couldn't very well tell him that what she had wanted was for him to send Tommy out looking for her and that the only reason she had come back at all was because she had realized it was soo soon. In time, yes, in good time Tommy would come for her; but not yet, she knew that, and first she would have to learn to think like a real woman, knowing the value of patience.

After that day things were not the same. Having sworn her love for Tommy, she did not need to change the daily pattern of her life. She did not follow him around the ranch anymore. When not in school, she stayed in her room or else helped Mother in the kitchen or around the house. She never saw Tommy except three times a day at the table. Except sometimes, out riding, she would catch a glimpse of him

working across the length of a wide field, just Tommy, a dark
spot at the edge of the world, and then that spot would
move and it would be Tommy waving at her.

She would wave back but ride no closer.

Only once did they really talk and that was by his
choosing and not hers. It happened exactly two weeks after
the Sunday when she had gone to his room. After dinner he
stopped her before she could reach the stairs and, taking her
by the arm, led her wordlessly out onto the porch. She sat on
the big iron swing and he leaned against the railing. Father, if
he wished, could easily see both of them from the chair in
the living room where he sat with his paper. See them, but
not hear them.

Tommy said, "I only wanted to tell you that I'm sorry. I
want you to know that I wasn't laughing at you. It was something else, something I can't explain now. What I do on
Sundays is so far from what you and your father seem to
think I do that I couldn't help laughing. But to answer your
question—and I think you deserve an answer after the way I
acted—the answer is no, I don't go there and I don't do that."

"I know," she said.

"You do?"

"I knew all along."

"Well . . . well then, fine."

"May I go inside now?" she asked.

"Yes, of course. I . . ."

She went, failing to hurry, proud of the way she had
handled him but afraid she could not maintain her dignity
too much longer. She was happy. He had noticed her, noticed that she was avoiding him, and felt bad because he had
caused it. Of course, he hadn't. He was wrong, but she
wasn't going to tell him differently. He would discover the
truth soon enough on his own.

For herself, Nadine was quite prepared to wait.

Chapter Three

Then it was harvest time. Ben Kincaid went to see a man named Worth—biggest grower in the valley—and Worth gave him a dozen extra hands. He brought the men home one evening, installed them in the orchard, and went out and started them picking the next morning.

For Nadine, the harvest meant that Tommy Bloome spent much more time each day around the house. Father was gone from dawn to dusk and Tommy now handled the routine chores of the ranch. Each afternoon he drove into town and purchased sufficient supplies not only for the family but also for the dozen pickers in the orchard.

At night, if they wished, the pickers were allowed to come down and sleep in the barn. Outside the doors, in a wide stretch of bare earth, they built their fires every night, cooking hasty meals over the open flames.

Nadine did not like the pickers—she never had. Most were foreign and even the few white men involved seemed like alien forms of life to her. Except once, a long time ago, she was hardly more than a child. Then she made good friends with a man who seemed younger and cleaner and better than the others. Mort was his name, and she had liked him a lot till Father asked so many questions about him that she had ended up crying. The next morning Mort wasn't there, and then she had hated him briefly for being so cruel as to leave without a word; but now, when she thought of him, which wasn't very often, she didn't hate him, because now she was old enough to understand.

She didn't talk to any of them now. In fact, when she could avoid it, she didn't go near them; they didn't smell good. Tommy said they didn't have any place to bathe.

"What about the creek?" she asked.

"That's three miles away."

"I go there all the time."

"On your horse."

"Well, I could walk if I had to. If it was the only way of getting clean."

"After picking apples for sixteen hours? I'd like to see you."

Mother did not like the pickers either and, at harvest time, she remained scrupulously indoors. Father said pickers were lazy and, if you didn't watch them, they'd steal more apples than they picked.

But what disturbed Nadine was Tommy: he didn't seem to mind them at all. They argued about this very often. Nadine told Tommy he ought to realize he was a better man than foreigners, Japs, and Negroes, but he said all men were equal, which she had learned in school and found hard to refute.

Her bedroom was located in the front of the house, and the window—pink lace curtains—overlooked the yard and barn. At night she could see the pickers clustered around their high campfires, eating, talking, drinking. The light was poor, so what she saw were dim shapes floating through a misty darkness of smoke, fire, and night. She saw Tommy the very first night. His red hair rendered his presence unmistakable. And he walked faster than the others; his movements were young, quick, brisk. He came out of the barn, went over to one group, and sat down. Later she saw him smoking cigarettes with another group. When she went to bed, he was still there.

The next night she saw him again. He came out as soon as the men finished eating, moving from fire to fire, group to group, man to man, as if he wished to speak to each of them in turn. Then Tommy and two of the men disappeared into the surrounding blackness. All three waved their hands and shook their heads, as if arguing. She didn't leave the window till way past midnight, but Tommy never came back.

She saw him the next morning at breakfast and looked closely for some clue that might help explain the events of the previous night. But nothing. His eyes, in fact, were shining bright and clear. Tommy didn't seem tired, but Nadine was.

"You don't look well," Mother said.

"I—I think I may be coming down with a cold."

"Perhaps you ought to stay home today."

"Oh, no." Guiltily. "No, I'll go."

The third night she was too tired to watch for long, though she did see Tommy come out and sit down with the men. This time there was definitely an argument, as one of the men, after a few moments, jumped up and rushed Tommy. Two others stepped in and broke up the fight. Tommy didn't leave after that. He started talking to one of the other men; Nadine thought the man might have been one of those Tommy had gone away with the other night. Then Tommy got up and moved into the darkness, and shortly afterward, a group of four followed him. Nadine wasn't able to stay awake and watch to see if he came back. As she drifted off, she wondered what Father thought about Tommy and the pickers. But did he even know? Father's bedroom was located way on the other side of the house, and he couldn't see the barn either from there or the living room. To her, the whole thing seemed strange and inexplicable. What could possibly be happening out there that caused men to argue and fight and disappear into the night?

For a full week this continued, Nadine watching every night. When the men finished eating, Tommy appeared. They talked and then some of them—once as many as ten but most often only three or four plus Tommy—went away. One night Nadine waited and waited, determined to discover the truth once and for all. It was past two o'clock before they came back—six men—but they all went straight into the barn and she briefly saw a light in Tommy's window. The next day in school she fell asleep at her desk and was made to stand in the corner most of the afternoon.

This same week she began to hear rumors. The kids at school were talking. She had so much on her mind, she didn't listen at first, but then her father started saying the same things and she realized it must be true. A strike. She didn't quite understand. Father said it meant the pickers demanded more money than the growers could afford to pay, but instead of understanding this and working for what they could get, the pickers refused to work or let anyone else work either; if someone else tried, even someone quite willing to work for whatever wages were offered, the old pickers would beat

them up or have them shot. With a strike the entire crop
might be allowed to rot on the trees and men would go
bankrupt because of the selfishness of a handful of men who
didn't even own land. Father said he was lucky because the
strike would not affect him like the big growers. Most likely,
if one did come, his trees would be cleared before the men
walked off. Last year some pickers had pulled a strike in
the vineyards and several big growers had actually gone
broke. The governor had sent soldiers down to make the men
return to work, but even then many had set out to sabotage
the remnants of the crop by starting fires and destroying fruit.
If a strike came here, it would upset the entire economy of
the valley, hurting everyone—farmer, worker, merchant—
alike.

While Father discussed the possibility of a strike, Tommy
remained silent. Once at supper Father asked him outright if
he had heard any of the men talking and Tommy said no,
because he never spent enough time with them to hear anything. Nadine was shocked but said nothing, not to Father or
Tommy. She couldn't very well go to him and say that she
had spied on him and knew he was lying when he said he
didn't know.

There was only one solution: she would have to follow
him.

She chose the Friday of the second week because the next
day was Saturday and she wouldn't have to get up early.
During the preceding days she had considered several courses
of action before finally deciding upon the one plan that
seemed most likely of success while not exposing her unnecessarily to the danger of discovery.

That night at supper—that Friday night—she said, "I really don't think I can eat this."

"What's wrong? You don't like chicken anymore?"

"I think I'm sick."

"You probably caught a cold," Mother said.

"No, not that. It started this afternoon."

"Oh," said Mother. "But don't you think you can eat a
little bit?"

She shook her head. "I'll try."

She did—tried not to eat it all. Anxiety had made her
famished. Father and Tommy were talking about baseball,

so she listened vaguely to them to keep her mind off her empty stomach. Father said he thought the San Francisco club had a good shot at the Coast League pennant this year. In the big leagues Father would have liked the Yankees to go all the way another time. Tommy shook his head and said, "No, the Senators." Father laughed. If not the Yankees, then it would have to be Connie Mack's A's. Walter Johnson all alone had never been enough to win it for Washington and besides Johnson was old and slowing down. "Maybe if Ruth breaks a leg and Pipp breaks an arm and Mark Koenig catches pneumonia, then the Yanks'll lose it. Otherwise, I can't see it."

Tommy was smiling, brash and confident as a button. "The Senators. And in the National League, the Giants again."

"I suppose you know who's going to win the series too?"

Tommy shook his head hastily and said of course he didn't.

Father wanted to argue about the St. Louis Cardinals and Hornsby. Nadine took this moment to slip away from the table. She had reached the stairs when Father called after her, "Where do you think you're going?"

"To bed."

"To rest?" Mother asked.

"To sleep."

So she had managed to pull it off beautifully. Upstairs in her room, she went straight to the window and looked out. The pickers were sitting around their fires, still eating. Knowing it would be a while before Tommy came, Nadine went over to her bed and crawled between the covers. It seemed like forever, but finally she heard Mother's footsteps trudging slowly up the stairs. Nadine shut her eyes and made her breath come regularly, as if she were sound asleep. Yellow light spilled suddenly across her face and she kept breathing— in and out, in and out—until the light went away. She listened to the steps dwindling down the stairs, then was up and out and back at the window.

The men were sitting much as she had left them, wiping their tin plates. Tommy must be in the barn. She looked up and saw—yes—the light burning in his window. That meant she still had time. But she would have to hurry. If she missed him tonight, it meant waiting another full week before trying again.

First she fixed the bed. She got some extra blankets from the closet and a big feather pillow and stuffed them carelessly underneath the bedcovers. Then she went to the door, opened it slightly, glanced back at the bed, nodded to herself, and went out.

She carried her shoes in one hand. The upstairs hallway was dark and empty. Father, she knew, would be in the living room and Mother in the kitchen. She walked on silent tiptoes.

Down the hall. Toward the stairs. Leaning over the railing, she surveyed the lower hall but saw nothing. Then she started down. Carefully, cautiously. A few of the boards creaked. She held her breath.

At the bottom, the carpet muffled her feet. She walked more boldly. When she reached the open doorway, she stopped. This led into the living room—and Father. She peeked around the corner, barely letting one eye show. She saw him. He sat in his favorite chair. He wasn't alseep. The evening paper from San Francisco—yesterday evening's actually—sat propped in his lap. His eyes were pointed down that way.

She wasn't sure. She thought his eyes looked half-closed and maybe if she waited he would fall asleep. Did she dare? At any moment Mother might choose to leave the kitchen back behind and, if she did, there was no way for Nadine to escape.

The doorway was six feet wide. She peeked again. Father hadn't moved. The slightest shift in his glance and he would surely see her.

She made up her mind. Now or never. She jumped, seeming to cover the whole distance in midair. On the other side, her feet, landing, thudded like gunshots.

She threw herself against the wall, her lungs gasping for air.

Then she waited.

Minutes seemed to pass, slowly lingering. Finally she made herself look. He was there; he hadn't moved.

The door leading outside was another three feet away. Earlier in the day she had oiled the lock and hinges. The door opened as silently as an angel. Smiling, she stepped outside.

Then, turning, she carefully closed the door. In silence. She had made it.

Now, with all her previously suppressed fear rising at once, she sprang forward, rushing across the yard, turning her steps so that she headed toward the barn.

She stopped at a point where the darkness was thick. But she could easily see the men and their fires from here. She put on her shoes. Tommy was not there yet. The men had finished eating and most were smoking hand-rolled cigarettes or cheap pipes.

It had to be a woman. Just because she lived on a farm and had never visited the city for more than a couple days at a time did not signify that she was hopelessly naïve. While formulating her plans, she had definitely made up her mind on this one point. A woman, a whore. Each night the men went out to visit her. Tommy too. But Nadine wanted to see this woman, she wanted to see what the men did with her, and Tommy too.

Here he came. She saw him emerge from the barn, passing not more than a half-dozen yards from where she stood, and cross to the men. Stopping beside one dwindling fire, he leaned over and spoke softly to another man. Then, standing, speaking loudly and clearly, directing his words toward no particular individual, he said, "Tonight is going to have to be the night."

"It's your butt," said one of the men.

Tommy pointed away toward the orchard. "All of our butts."

Shortly afterward, he went away. Alone.

For Nadine, waiting now was difficult but necessary. Others would soon be following Tommy. He went first but never alone. She couldn't budge until all of them had gone first.

Here they came. A big bunch tonight. They moved past her hiding place. Nadine counted. Five, eight, ten, twelve men.

She went right after them, following the sound of their footsteps, crossing the deep dark fields. Behind, the flames of the fires dwindled, then disappeared. The house was gone too. She was alone with the men ahead of her. The only illumination came from the sky, the stars and a half-full moon.

She couldn't see the men. She walked slowly, allowing them to move farther and farther ahead. Toward the orchard. That was obviously where they were leading her. Why? she wondered. Was it a good place? Dark? Mysterious? No one would find them there.

Ahead: a light.

She stopped and stared. It was a fire. Burning at the edge of the orchard. She hurried closer and saw the men she had been following enter the circle of fire. And Tommy—yes, she saw him—he was already there.

Creeping closer, she circled the fire and crouched down in the moist dirt of the orchard. A wide apple tree hung over her head, one long branch dangling in front of her nose; she counted three apples.

Around the fire, more men had gathered; they must have arrived while she wasn't looking. She tried to count, but they kept moving, circling, standing, then sitting. She couldn't keep them straight. At least thirty, she guessed. Maybe forty. Pickers. Nearly all were white men too, though even these were brown and wrinkled and wore patchy beards and torn soiled clothing. Forty scarecrows, that's how it looked, dancing around a big fire.

But there shouldn't be that many. She knew her theory— woman, whore—was no longer valid. But, if not that, then why? What did they want here?

Then she saw Tommy. He passed through the crowd and mounted the flat stump of a fallen tree. He waved his hands. Silence fell. A few men sat down; most remained standing, ready to listen.

Tommy spoke. Nadine tried to concentrate on what he was saying but she was too excited; his words did not seem clear. She fought to comprehend. Strike. That was it. Tommy was telling the men they ought to strike. No, there was more to it than that: they were going to strike. Tomorrow. At ten o'clock.

"The signs—everything we will need—they ought to be here tomorrow," Tommy said. "As soon as we walk out, there will be people to help us establish our lines. After ten tomorrow, I'm telling you, there won't be an apple picked in this valley. If the growers get hungry and want to do their own picking"—laughter—"then we won't stop them. Maybe they'll learn a thing or two having to work with their own hands for a change." More laughter. "But that's the only way it'll happen—if we stay together."

"What about us?" asked a man. "When we get hungry?"

"You haven't been out here before," Tommy said.

"No, I haven't."

"Then ask a man who has. I can't take time to answer every question. Not tonight. We've covered all this before. It's too late to change anything now; we've gone too far. The strike is set. Ten o'clock. Pass the word. That's all I've got to say." Tommy waved his hands in a gesture of dismissal.

But one man shouted, "My people say they can't go!"

"Then get them to go," Tommy said. "That's your job."

"It's no use," the man said. "I've been talking and talking to them. But, hell, half can't even understand English. And they're scared of the cops, scared of starving. Most of them were in this mess last year and they got beat and beat bad. I've got a Mexican woman there whose husband got clubbed to death. They listen to her more than me."

"But you're their representative, right?"

"So you keep telling me."

"O.K., then listen," said Tommy. "Let me tell you how it is." He had everyone's firm attention now, including Nadine's. "For weeks we've been meeting out here every night. Some nights we've been here till four and five in the morning. Everything's been discussed and fought and argued. And everything has been voted on, ain't that right?"

The crowd agreed that was right.

Tommy said, "So it really comes down to this. You men are supposed to represent all the pickers in this valley. You said you wanted to strike. That means they want to strike, too. I hope that's the way it is because, I'm telling you, nobody's going to back out now. One thing about a strike, any strike, no one man can be himself. We're all part of one big animal, a beast, a hungry beast. It's the same as a bear if one of his toes was to decide not to go hunting with the rest of him. If the bear let his toe do that, then the bear would starve. Instead, he'll bite off that toe and spit it out. We have to do the same. Every man is in this strike together. When one man says no, then all of us must also say no. When all of us say yes, then that one man had better say yes too. Otherwise we'll go right down and bite him off and spit him out on the ground. Is that clear?"

It was. A few men cheered. Most simply turned away, speaking softly among themselves. Tommy remained on the peak of his stump.

When he was alone, he jumped down and went over to heap dirt upon the fire.

Then he headed across the fields toward the house.

Nadine followed.

Nadine kept Tommy in sight. He was walking quickly and she had to hurry to keep pace. A breeze ran through her hair, lashing loose strands gently against her face. Tommy moved through the moonlight, occasionally flickering out of sight for brief times. Sometimes, distantly, she overheard other voices, anonymous footsteps. A car engine coughed. A man shouted. A woman screamed.

"Nadine."

She stopped and said, "Tommy?"

He stepped from behind a tree. "I thought I heard . . ." He shook his head.

She glanced down at his hand, seeing in the moonlight the shadow of a knife.

"Are you going to kill me?" she asked.

He shook his head and pocketed the knife. "No."

She rushed to explain: "I saw you going away. Every night, from my window. I—I'm sorry, but I had to know. I thought . . . a woman . . . I didn't know about the strike."

"But now you do."

"Yes, yes, I heard."

"So what are you going to do?"

She shook her head, unable to answer.

"Don't you care?" he asked.

"I care about my father," she said quickly. "He doesn't—"

"I care about him too," Tommy said. "I'm sorry if he gets hurt. But it's the others who matter."

She didn't try to reply. They stood silently regarding each other for a long moment. Then Tommy reached out and took her hand.

"Come on. There's no use standing here. Let's go home."

"O.K.," she said. They were quite alone now. No sounds penetrated their isolation, nothing. Tommy led the way.

"I won't tell," she suddenly said.

"All right," Tommy said. He let go of her hand and moved ahead.

She sprang after him, grabbing his arm, causing him to turn. Their eyes met.

"I really won't," she said.

"Why?"

"Because I love you."

She couldn't see his expression in the dim grayness of the night. "No," he said.

"I do—I told you I did. Don't you remember?"

"I remember."

She waited.

Finally he raised a hand and touched her lips with his palm.

"Should I say it again?" she asked.

"Go home, Nadine. I don't care what you say." His hand had not moved.

"Why?"

"It's too late to stop us now. We've gone too far."

"I don't care!" Suddenly her voice was angry. She grabbed his arm and forced his hand away from her lips. "It doesn't matter to me."

"Do you really mean that?"

"Yes!" she cried. "Yes, of course I do. Oh, Tommy."

He held her in his arms. His lips touched hers. Strong lips, his, cheek upon cheek. Arms, strong, around her. They fell to the ground. She kissed him. He kissed her. It was wet on the ground and the earth shook and the sky whirled and he cried out.

She cried, "Oh, God! Tommy, my Tommy! I love you! Oh, I do; yes, I do, I do!"

There was more. After this, much more, but Nadine never recollected beyond that sacred moment in the pasture. For her it had ended there.

Stories always did.

But now it was dark. And Sam had not come.

She was beginning to think he never would.

She got up from the hard floor of the roof and went slowly to the door that led down the stairs. When she reached the apartment, she opened the door and went inside and wasn't the least surprised to find that it was empty and Sam was gone. He had taken his clothes too. She felt nothing. She sat down on the broken couch and wondered how she was supposed to feel. Lost? Hurt? In pain? She tried to speak aloud, but all that came out was "Tommy, Tommy Bloome." Nothing else.

And Tommy was dead.

Chapter Four

Tommy Bloome, neck muscles tensed with the strain, raised his face out of the water. He couldn't hold it there; the effort was too immense. He remembered the rock. When he fell, it had been there. He tried to find it again, using the side of his face like a groping hand. Ah. There it was. He laughed, coughed, and laid his face upon the flat smooth side of the rock. He breathed. At last. The air tasted clean and sweet and remarkably pure. He used his mouth. His nose, he thought, was broken.

Maybe he should try to move now. Get out of this ditch. Yes, somehow, sometime, some way, out of the ditch. But not now. If he tried now, he wasn't going to make it and failure was more than he could bear. Better to wait. Breathe. Living was good enough. He liked to hear the rasping noise his throat made as the air stuck halfway down. He was safe now. The others wouldn't hear for a while and he was safe from the ones who had done this. The bastards. They had done their job, and now it was his friends, his comrades, whom he must fear. They might want to do to him what the vigilantes in Chehalis in 1919 had done to Wesley Everest. Did Wesley Everest exist in this world? Some men did and some did not, he knew. Tommy did not want to suffer that kind of pain for anything. He had already died once, and if he had to die a second time, he wanted it to be quiet and quick. But if the pickers got to talking and figured out who they ought to blame for losing their jobs, then they'd come for him. He had better move.

He couldn't.

His only mistake had been running. He should have stood and faced them straight out. That wouldn't have saved him but the ferocity of their attack might have been lessened. When a man is running wildly away, then it's easy to pick up

49

a big rock and send it crashing into the back of his head. And once he's down, blood mixing with the earth, then there's nothing to standing and kicking and clubbing. By the time he's out cold, it's even easier. You kick him because he's not a man anymore—not even a cornered animal—but just a hunk of dead meat.

Then it's simple to say, "All right, two grab his feet."

Into the ditch he goes.

And if he doesn't wake up, if he happens to die, then there's still no worry in it for you. The county coroner has held office for twenty years and knows enough to point out that the deceased was walking through the pasture late at night (drunk, no doubt) and forgot to look where he was going and fell into the ditch and hit his head on a rock and died. As far as the cuts and bruises and broken ribs and mashed nose and crushed groin are concerned—well, those are the odd details that invariably arise to clutter the simple facts in the simple case of the death of a simple man.

Accidental drowning per misadventure: that's the verdict.

But Tommy Bloome wasn't dead. He kept reminding himself of that. And if he hadn't been screwing the kid. That was the biggest mistake he'd made. If he hadn't started screwing her, this would never have happened. No, he corrected himself, it would have happened two weeks ago instead, when she told her father everything she'd overheard in the orchard. At least this way the strike had got started. And that was something. Wasn't it?

Oh, hell. What was the use of thinking this way? No man can think in terms of what might have been when his whole existence is predicated upon the fact of one great huge should never have been. He was Tommy Bloome, a dead man. Shot dead twenty-three years from now. A man of twenty-four born six months ago. Born twice six months ago.

"Bloome," said a voice.

Huh? Who?

"Bloome, can you talk?"

Something warm touched his forehead.

"Bloome, if you can't talk, don't try." Another warm touch at his side.

"Who . . ." Tommy managed, "who are you?"

"A friend."

"Get me . . ."

"Yes, I will. Don't talk now. Just wait."

Hands lifted him up. He felt the ditch dwindling away. The stars. The moon. He was lying on his back.

"Can you get up?" asked the voice.

"I— Yes." He thought he saw a face up there. A big yellow round ball of a face. It kept moving, shifting. No, that wasn't a face; it was the moon. No, it wasn't the moon either; it was a lantern.

"I'm going to carry you," said the voice. "This will hurt, so hang on."

It didn't hurt at all. That was funny because nothing had hurt since the moment the rock struck the back of his head. Even the men kicking him, he hadn't felt a thing.

He was being carried across the pasture. He tried to relax and ride. His jaw bounced lightly against the man's back. His feet dangled loosely in the air.

"What's your name?" he asked.

"Ennis. Bob Ennis. It doesn't matter."

"Where are you taking me?"

"Right here."

He seemed to turn head over heels and thought for a moment he was falling into the ditch again. But when he landed, it was something cold, hard, slick.

"Just listen to me now," Bob Ennis was saying. "I'm going to put a blanket over you. If we reach the main highway without being stopped, we should be all right. The growers won't bother us. They took care of you. But the pickers won't ever cool down. We're going to have to drive fast and hard and not let anybody or anything stop us. It'll be rough. So I want you to lay still. Don't move, don't say a word. Understand?"

"O.K.," Tommy said.

"Good. Now here goes, now hold on."

The car started up. It was black, very black, with the blanket over his face. He was lying on the back seat of the car. It moved forward, slowly at first, then gathering speed. Time would pass the fastest if he could fall asleep. He tried. At least he knew where he was going now: he was going away. The car began to bounce. Bad road. A vicious pain burned in his chest. There was another inside his skull. He heard noises outside. Men yelling? Then they were gone.

His thoughts continued to surprise him. The image that loomed largest in his memory was one he shouldn't even remember: Nadine. He ought to hate her. If the pickers had not caught them together two nights ago, the strike might still be going. They should have trusted him. He couldn't bring himself in all honesty to blame her. He had used her, that was all; and it wasn't her fault it hadn't worked. And she had loved him. That was the most amazing thing of all.

I bet she's crying her eyes out this minute, he thought. And that made him want to laugh. He didn't. Maybe later, maybe when he woke up. That would be a good time to laugh, he thought.

When Tommy awoke, the morning sun stood right above his eyes. He blinked and rolled over. He was still in the car. The blanket lay in a heap on the floor.

Tommy sat up and groaned. Every muscle in his body ached. His chest throbbed. He raised his hands and saw that they were covered with blood. He touched his nose and felt the shattered bone. Then he smelled something: cooking, coffee.

He turned and looked out the car window but could see nothing but trees. A real forest extending endlessly away over rising hills. He got out of the car, testing his legs before daring to walk forward.

He followed the smell of the coffee, circling the car. There were more trees here but also a narrow dirt road that turned a corner about a hundred feet farther down. Beside the road he found a campfire. The man seated before the flames was big, strong-looking, perhaps thirty. He wore an old pair of blue overalls and a big straw hat that concealed his eyes from the sun.

"Hello, Bloome," he said, spying Tommy.

"I forget your name." Tommy crouched beside the fire.

"Bob Ennis."

"Well, thanks. For pulling me out of the ditch."

"Have some coffee. It's all we've got."

"I will." Tommy accepted a tin cup and sipped slowly. "Where are we? This can't be the valley."

"No, we're in the mountains. I thought going east would fool them."

"Did it?"

"More or less. I had to plow through a line of them near Worth's farm."

"Hurt anyone?"

"Not especially."

Tommy nodded. The coffee had cooled now. He downed a large gulp. And it was strong. "Why did you do it? Save my life?"

Ennis shook his head and stood quickly. "Let's take a walk. There's a creek down below. You can wash some of the blood off and I'll tell you."

"O.K.," Tommy said.

They followed a path through the trees. It wound downward. A cool breeze rippled lightly past them.

"What's the hurry?" Ennis asked, struggling to match Tommy's pace.

"These trees. I'm not used to them." But he slowed down.

"You didn't belong on that farm."

"I worked on one when I was a kid."

"But you never tried to start a strike."

"No."

"You shouldn't have tried back there either."

"Why not? They were ready for it. They—"

"If they'd been ready, they would have won," Ennis said.

The stream lay at the bottom of the path, a yard wide, a few inches deep. The water was very cold. Ennis drew a red-and-black bandanna out of a pocket and passed it to Tommy, who dipped one end in the stream and washed his face. Some of the blood, caked to his skin, had to be loosened with a fingernail. The water soothed the aching in his temples. Only his ribs really hurt him now and he was ready to talk. He leaned back, sitting on the bank.

"Want to talk?" he asked.

Ennis nodded. "Sure. Why don't you start off by telling me your real name?"

Tommy felt a momentary fear running up his spine. But this man could not possibly know. "Tommy Bloome is my real name."

"Then that explains why none of us ever heard of you."

"Who is us?"

"San Francisco."

"Well, I knew some party people in Stockton."

"We don't have any people in Stockton. A different faction. Did they send you here?"

Tommy shook his head. "It was my own idea. I got a couple of them to help me at the beginning—signs and the like—but they got scared when things got hot and ran off."

"They were smart," Ennis said.

Tommy shrugged. "I did my best."

"That means nothing. That valley is the tightest place in the state. You never had a chance."

"I'm not so sure. If we'd kept the scabs out of the orchards, I think we could have broke them."

"How?"

"Any way. Sabotage. Picket lines that won't crack at the first sign of force. Guns, for all I care. Anything except what they did. Which was fold up and fade away."

"If you'd fought, the army would have come in."

"So? At least we'd have made the papers."

"For a man so young," Ennis said, "you seem to have an awful urge to die."

Tommy couldn't help grinning at that. "Not me. But maybe dying is better than living in some ways."

"I used to think that way too. But I'm not a kid anymore. I've been slamming my head against the stone wall of U.S. capitalism since 1912, so I know what I'm talking about. I've been to college. I studied at the University of Washington in Seattle for two years. Before the war, I was an I.W.W., so I know something about fighting too. I got drafted. Some men resisted. I said I'd go. What better cross section of dispossessed America than a conscripted army. I went in. I went to France. And what did I do when I got there? I shot Germans. For all I knew, or cared, every damn one of them could have been a good socialist back in Berlin. But they were trying to kill me. What the books said didn't matter. When I got out after the Armistice, I was a different man. That's when I went to college. But old habits don't change and I got involved in the Seattle general strike in 1919. From there, I wandered down here and somehow got into the party in '20. But I'm not a fool. You don't have to remind me there was a revolution in Russia and almost one in Germany. I've been to both places. I went to Moscow two years ago and met Lenin and had dinner with Trotsky, but I still say there isn't a country on Earth that's going to have a revolution till the people—and I mean the real basic people, not a few malcontents like you and me—are ready for it. And this country ain't ready. There's too much loose money floating around. Everybody thinks they're going to get a slice of the pie and enough get it so the others keep hoping. They are fools. They lie to themselves. If I could snap my fingers and show them the real facts, you bet I would. But I can't. And if you think you can, then one time the goons will forget to stop beating on your head before they crack your skull and that will be the end of you and nothing will be any different with you dead than it was when you were alive."

"Are you through?" Tommy asked.

"I try to keep my speeches fairly short," Ennis said.

"Then listen to mine."

"O.K."

"Well, to start, you've got me wrong. I'm not some kid who's read the manifesto and thinks he ought to go out and start a real shooting revolution. In fact, I agree pretty much with every word you just said except for one thing. You seem to think what's true now is going to stay true forever and that ain't true. Do you remember what a depression is?"

"Of course I do."

"There's not so much loose money in the pie then, is there?"

"Perhaps not. But there have been thirteen depressions since the end of the Civil War and not one revolution."

"And if there's another?"

"A few people go hungry. Then it ends and nobody remembers till the next one hits."

"But what if it doesn't end? What happens if there's ten or fifteen million people all over this country out of work and starving? What happens if Wall Street falls on its face and bankers start jumping out windows because they're going broke too? What happens if there aren't any jobs for anybody and the banks have folded, taking people's savings down with them, and the farmers can't sell their crops for more than a penny a bushel because nobody in the cities has any money for food? And what happens if this depression keeps going—it doesn't stop, it gets worse and worse for a whole year, then two years, and pretty soon five years? And the President—say, he's like the man we've got now—and all he can do is sit at his desk, saying over and over that it's going to get better, that people have to be patient, but it doesn't get better; it keeps getting worse and worse. You tell me, Ennis, what's going to happen then?"

"It won't happen that way. Not here."

"I'm telling you it is going to happen."

"What is this?" Ennis shook his head and chuckled. "I thought you were a Red, not a prophet out of the Bible."

"I'm both. Who knows what I am? I'm just telling you this: when this depression comes, there's going to be a revolution in this country. And there's two ways that revolution can turn; it can go left or right. And if you think things are bad now, just imagine this country being run by a pack of two-bit Mussolinis, a bunch of Mitchell Palmers, how are you going to like that then?"

"Keep talking," Ennis said, deadly serious now.

"I've only got one more thing to say, and that's this: I want our side to win. I don't care how many son-of-a-bitching fruitpickers got to lose their balls in the process, because it'll be nothing compared to what'll happen if we don't win."

"When's it going to happen? Next year? You better tell me that too."

"I'll tell you the truth," Tommy said. He pretended to consider. "Five years maybe. But another five years before the revolution will break out."

"Ten years is a hell of a long time. Aren't you starting kind of early?"

"Is there a better way? How long did it take Lenin?"

"Are you comparing yourself to him?"

"I'll let you do that." Tommy stood up. "Come on, we better get moving. We both made our speeches, now it's time to check the car."

Ennis stood up and followed Tommy obediently toward the trail. Neither needed to speak. When they reached the car, Ennis sat behind the wheel.

"You want me to drop you in Stockton?" he asked.

"No, I'm through up there."

"Well, where?"

"San Francisco's fine with me. If you don't mind the company."

"Not at all. In fact, I've got a friend who's a good doctor and doesn't ask questions."

"That's just what I need."

Ennis let the car warm up, then turned down the road, weaving through the tree-covered hills. When they reached the main road, Tommy leaned over and said, "You were right about one thing back there, Bob."

"Well, thanks for that."

"This country isn't for me. I belong in the city. When the revolution comes, that's where it'll happen. It might start out here—the farmers always got the worst end of every stick—but the fighting will be in the cities. That's where we're going to have to win."

"Sure," Ennis said, agreeably.

"You still don't believe me, do you?"

"I don't know," Ennis said.

But Tommy didn't care. Ennis could believe if he wished, but Tommy had a force on his side far stronger than simple belief or disbelief. He had history. And history did not lie. It did not lie but it could be changed. And he would be the one who would do the changing. He hadn't been sure until the moment he began to answer Ennis, and then he had known for certain what his mission in life was going to be. He, Tommy Bloome, was going to change history or—there was no other alternative—he would die trying.

He shut his eyes and began to dream.

Chapter Five

Robert Benjamin Franklin Ennis belonged to that select circle of men who possess the ability to consume vast amounts of alcoholic liquor without displaying any of the common outward signs of drunkenness. In Ennis' particular case, this ability, beyond a certain sluggishness of thought, extended into his interior life as well. Ennis had developed and refined this talent over a period of many years during which the circumstances of his life had often required him to keep a clear head. But he did like to drink; he had a difficult time living without a sip now and then. He preferred bourbon, which he drank straight, without ice. And there was one other conditon, not necessarily a symptom of intoxication but a thing that did occur only when Ennis had been drinking: he talked. Normally an exceedingly silent man, his lips, after a half-dozen drinks, would mysteriously open, as if disengaged by some form of magic, and his tongue would begin flapping like a loose shoelace.

This time Bob Ennis had been drinking (and talking) for more than twenty-six consecutive hours. He was a tall man with a huge chest and arms and a belly that was big without being fat. His hair rested on the back of his head like an eagle's crest; his clothes were old, tattered, those of a farmer or fisherman. As he talked, he kept both elbows propped on the bar and did not move except when it was time for another belt. He had been here at Molly's ever since the night of the fourth. He glanced at the clock above the bar mirror. Five minutes after twelve. That meant it was now July 6, 1947, and Tommy Bloome had been dead two days.

Except for Molly, Ennis was alone. He had arrived during a slack drinking time and Molly had not demurred when he'd asked her to close the bar and keep it closed. Her full name was Molly Killian and he had known her since San

Francisco in the twenties when she had been working in a middle-class saloon on Pacific Street. He had given her the money to buy this bar in '35 and Tommy had signed the license personally. Ennis squinted at the parchment mounted behind the bar but failed to make out anything but an indecipherable scrawl that could have said Jack Benny as well as Tommy Bloome. Well, Molly Killian—there was no doubt of this—stood as the love of his life, and the only competition she had ever had in this regard came from Tommy Bloome, but Ennis did not think there was ever a time when he had actually loved Tommy. In the beginning he had liked him—they were friends—and then he had admired him, worshiped him, and finally it had largely been pity and compassion. But love? He did not think so. With Tommy, life was never so simple as that.

"Dead," Ennis said aloud, and he reached for his glass.

Molly was seated at the opposite end of the bar. She frowned at the word.

Ennis swallowed deeply. "Give me another," he said, pushing the empty glass across.

Molly nodded and filled the glass from a bottle behind the bar. She wasn't drinking with him anymore; she had had sense enough to quit last night. He thought all the years had treated her pretty well. Her eyes were as bright and green as ever, and her hair was still coal black. Underneath her eyes, the skin was white, clean, unwrinkled. The only creases in her flesh lay down below, around her jawline and throat; her hands were raw and red but they always had been. She was a tiny wisp of a woman, but tough as a bug, and, as he had recalled earlier, he did love her.

The liquor was tasteless. The last time any of it had affected him was last night. He couldn't even feel his tongue anymore. The liquor went down as dry and cold as tap water.

"Again?" Molly said, suddenly.

Ennis glanced up. "Again, what?"

"Moping," she said.

"I'll mope when the bottle's gone."

"It is. I'll have to feed you the legal stuff now."

"That's warm water."

"I have Scotch."

"No. It has to be bourbon. That's an American whisky. When Stalin dies, I'll drink vodka. For Tommy, it has to be bourbon."

"You could go there, you know. To Russia. They'd take you."

"It's too cold. Besides, to get there from here I'd need wings." He frowned at her suspiciously. "What's wrong? Afraid they'll catch me here and take your franchise away?"

She shook her head, refusing to take offense. I'll lose that no matter what. And if they catch you here, they'll kill me anyway."

He nodded. "I'm sorry."

She pointed at his glass. "You know, Bob, you can't keep that up much longer. Besides, what's the point? He's dead. That won't bring him back."

"God bless him," Ennis said, swallowing the remainder of the drink.

"You bless him. Not me. I didn't like him."

"You never knew him.".

"Maybe so."

"You bet so." He tried to nod, but his jaw slipped away from him and nearly struck the surface of the bar. He stared down at his glass. "I think I'd better go now. Believe it or not, I'm getting drunk."

"No," she said. "You can't go out like that. Eat something first. I've seen you drink twice this much but you've got to eat."

"Who's hungry?" he asked. Then, suddenly, he smiled. "I remember a guy I knew in San Francisco in the twenties who drank ten times as much as I ever did. He never quit, never, from dawn to midnight and beyond. Drinking was fun back then. It was serious stuff. This guy was a Red and he used to say he was assisting in the overthrow of a rotten system by violating the laws, but the only law I ever saw him break was Prohibition. But here, look here." He reached down and untied one shoe and held it up where she could see the sole. "See here, right below the toe. This guy's shoe had a big dent in it there. You know what it came from? From resting on the damn barrail all day. He drank so much he wore a dent in his shoe." He laughed shrilly. "And when they buried him in '38, I went to his funeral and, yep, there was the dent in the shoes they buried him in."

"How did he die?" Molly asked.

"Shut your mouth," Ennis said angrily.

"If he died in '38, I bet it wasn't drink. What happened? Didn't your Tommy think he was funny?"

"I said for you to shut up." He pointed a finger at her chest, then added, in a murmur, "What Tommy did that year was necessary."

"That's what they say about Hitler and the Jews."

"Hitler's still alive. Talk about him all you want. But Tommy's dead and before he was dead he was beaten, so why not leave him alone? Lowrey's killed more men than Tommy ever dreamed of, so call Lowrey a son of a bitch but leave Tommy alone. He was sorry for what he did."

"Bullshit," she said.

"He told me. How do you know so much? You don't know anything."

"Neither do you. He kicked you in the face and you're still loving him."

"Shut up," he said, making a fist. He gazed bemusedly at the white knuckles. "Not another word."

"Fine by me." She went down to the other end of the bar and, finding a damp towel, began to wipe the surface. Ennis, left alone, began to think he ought to try to sober up before they came to kill him. He didn't especially want to die drunk. If death had been more certain, he would surely have made an effort. But he thought he was safe here. As long as he stayed here, they probably wouldn't find him. So he decided to continue drinking for a little while longer; getting sober could come later.

"I want to stay alive to see the funeral," Ennis called to Molly. "When he's in the ground, then I can join him."

"The funeral's Tuesday in Washington. You can't make it."

"Why not? Everybody else is going to be there. People Tommy never knew. Ministers and commissioners and administrators and ambassadors. What right do they have going there? And Rachel. I can see her: dressed in black, sobbing her heart out, making sure the radio catches every note. And Lowrey will be there at the head of the parade.

I ought to go there. Tommy deserves to have one real friend on the spot. They'll kill me, of course, but I'd still like to go."

"You know too much," she said.

He laughed. "You bet I did. Not as much as they think, but plenty. I know about China and Poland and Africa. All those places Tommy's supposed to've been since 1940 and never came within five thousand miles of. Wasn't Tommy supposed to have been in Africa when he died? That must have been embarrassing for them."

"No, he came back last spring."

"Too bad. I like to think of Lowrey sweating to come up with the right lie. What I can't forget is all those winters, Tommy and I freezing our asses off in that cabin, the ocean roaring just outside the door. I don't think Tommy said more than twenty words a day to me all those years, but it was still the only time when I really got to know him. When I first met him, I thought he was a dumb kid. Next thing I knew he was a great visionary, a brilliant man. But it was only in the cabin that I really got to know him. I remember one time, about six months after we won the revolution, Tommy and I were sitting in his office. We were working on some army reports dealing with the mopping up, and it was a pretty impressive moment because both of us knew we couldn't lose now; I remember I turned to Tommy and said, 'I have never asked you for one thing since this thing started but now there is something.' He said, 'Name it, Bob. Any position you want, it's yours for the asking, but I'll tell you the truth—I was hoping you wouldn't ask. What I'd like is to have you around as a sort of special adviser. I need one man near me I can really trust. I'll give you a title—Special Consultant to the First Director—but I need you, Bob.' And I said, 'It's nothing like that, Tommy. I don't want a job or position or title or money. All I want is to be the man who writes your biography. You're going to need one someday, whether you want it or not, and I'd like to be the guy who does the writing.' I remember when I said that how I couldn't help remembering how I'd first come into his life as the man who'd picked him out of a ditch. But he said, 'I'm sorry, Bob,' and he meant it. He said, 'Bob, I'd like to have you do it, but it wouldn't work. There is no story to my life—nothing to tell—and there never will be. Outside this particular time and place, I am nothing. I am not even a man, Bob; I am a set of ideas and concepts. That is the way it must be and that is the way it will be.' I knew he meant that; I told him so and I never asked him again."

"Well, you must have known something about him." She was seated across from Ennis now, though neither was bothering to drink.

"Not much. No more than you or anyone else. It was like his life started the day I pulled him out of that irrigation ditch. Oh, he was around before that. He'd known a few party people in Stockton that winter. He said he was born in Chicago, but you won't find his name on the records there. Don't ask me. He never talked about those years."

Molly was laughing now. "I always thought you knew," she said. "I thought the secrecy was a fake. Making a mystery man out of Bloome. Impressing the ignorant masses. Like Christ, how twenty years—thirty—most of his life, nobody knows what he did, where he was. You want another."

"All right."

"This will be legal."

"I can bear it."

She removed a bottle from beneath the bar. The label represented the stars and stripes flapping in the breeze.

Ennis accepted his drink, frowned, then swallowed in a gulp. "Have one yourself."

"What the hell," said Molly. She poured a second glass.

Ennis went on, "There were a few things I learned about him that nobody else knows to this day, but that was only because I was around him for so many years. One thing happened in the twenties—it must have been in 1927—in Chicago. Tommy and I had gone there to attend a party meeting—the national convention, in fact. It was the first time either of us had been out of California on party business, so it turned out to be a big moment for Tommy; he became famous for the first time. Anyway, we showed up with all the California people in our pocket. We were known out there and Tommy had already decided—not telling anybody but me—that he was going to make a stab at the leadership. He didn't expect to make it—and he didn't—but it started getting his name mentioned in the same breath as Browder and Foster, and when it was time for a change in leadership, people turned his way.

"But I was telling you about something else. Tommy and I shared a room in a cheap hotel around the Loop. The convention was being held a little down the street, some Polish Veterans Hall, something like that, and we were supposed to attend a committee meeting one morning. We left the hotel as if we were going straight to the hall, but when we reached the doors, Tommy took my arm and said he didn't give a damn what Stalin wanted us to believe this year but had another thing he wanted to do. I got the impression he would just as soon see me go inside, but I ended up tagging at his heels. He went to a county office, the place where the vital records are kept, and went to one room, telling the woman at the desk, 'My name is David O'Mara and I'd like a copy of my son's birth certificate.' 'When was your son born, Mr. O'Mara?' she asked. Tommy said, 'October 16, 1923,' and I was puzzled, because I knew October 16 was also his birthday. The woman asked for the boy's name and Tommy said it was Timothy. Anyway, the woman went away and while she was gone I got to thinking. I remembered Tommy always said he came from Chicago, so maybe this kid was really his and the birthday was a coincidence. Maybe Tommy had got some girl pregnant and that was why he had come to California in the first place. And he had changed his name to Bloome— that made sense too, especially if she was looking for him. But then the woman came back with a funny look and said there was no record of any such child being born in Chicago on that day and how she had checked on September 16 and November 16 and maybe Tommy had the wrong year. He agreed that was possible but didn't ask her to look anymore, but instead turned on his heel and out we went. He had a huge smile on his face and I remember he turned and told me, 'Bob, I just learned something. History. It's not always the same. It can change just like anything else.' I started to ask what the hell he was talking about but I could tell from his manner he wasn't going to answer, so I said nothing. I don't know what he meant to this day, but I have a funny feeling it might be important."

"So he either had a kid or he didn't," Molly said. "That doesn't sound so important."

"Well, actually, there's more," said Ennis. "This next happened a long time later—after the revolution, in fact. My office was located right outside Tommy's door and I saw every sheet of paper he saw. Well, one day I was thumbing through a stack of papers and I came across this list that was about three pages long and on it was the full name and address of what must have been every Timothy O'Mara in the country. You remember that was supposed to be the name of the kid Tommy was checking on in Chicago. I picked up the list and carried it into his office and laid it down. He saw it, picked it up, read it through, then said the way he always did, 'Thanks, Bob,' without volunteering a thing. I respected his privacy and left it at that, but I do know for a fact he had the FBI check out every name on that list because the reports started coming over my desk the next week, but if Tommy ever found what he was looking for, he didn't bother to tell me."

"Or else he didn't find out till after you were gone." Molly was working on a second drink. "After he kicked your ass out cold."

"I quit," Ennis said.

"You were purged."

"No."

"He asked you to quit, didn't he?"

"I was going to do it anyway."

"Because you couldn't stomach what he was doing."

"It was necessary. I know that now."

"Murder is murder, necessary or not."

"Have it your own way," he said sullenly.

"Well, don't pout. He didn't kill you. He killed everybody else he could get hold of, but not you. I guess that's what you call friendship."

"Well," Ennis said with a philosophical nod, "it doesn't much matter. I won't be living very much longer in any event. But the past is the past, and Tommy's dead and I'm alive and I think we ought to remember the good he accomplished. You can't deny him that. What about the Depression? Did you enjoy that? Would you like to have Baker back in the White House. How about Herbert Hoover? You want them, I'll find them for you. Baker has an apartment in

New York City. Lenin shot the tsar, but Tommy never did any of that."

"How about Hoover?"

"He's alive. John Nance Garner too. Remember Franklin Roosevelt, Teddy's cousin who was the governor. He died down in Georgia two years ago. Had polio and was living O.K. on a government social pension. If you ask me, we've been pretty fair to all of them."

"They couldn't hurt you. Nobody would ever have wanted any of them back. Have another drink."

He accepted the flag-decorated bottle and poured his own drink. His eyes were threatening to shut of their own accord and he was beginning to feel as if he were trapped inside a cocoon. Well, maybe it was time. Thirty hours. Forty or more since he'd last slept. He stifled a yawn, then leaned back, stretched his legs, straightened his spine.

"You ought to go to bed," Molly said.

"I'm beginning to think you're right. I'm drunk enough now so that I'm sober again."

"Finish that one, then go."

"I think I will." He took a deep, satisfying swallow. He still couldn't taste the liquor. "Play some music," he told Molly. "Something soft, easy on the head. Sinatra." There was a dark jukebox in one corner of the barroom.

"Better not," Molly said. "Somebody might hear."

"Let them."

"No," she said. "You can say that, but I'm too old to die yet."

"Maybe you should kick me out."

She smiled sympathetically. "I'd rather you went to bed."

"I will. If you'll smile like that again."

"Like this?" She puckered her lips, making tiny dimples in her cheeks.

"Close," he said.

"It's not so easy to do as it once was."

"Nothing is."

Both their glasses were empty. There, for a moment, Bob Ennis had completely forgotten about Tommy Bloome. Molly had done that—her smile. It had brought back the past, a better past, his own past for a change, and not simply Tommy's.

"Remember how I said Tommy could see the future," he said.

"I remember."

"How the first time I met him he told me about the Depression, the whole thing, the revolution too. I just remembered one thing he missed: Newton Baker."

"Why?" she said. "Did he think it was going to be Roosevelt? Most people did."

"Yes and no. That was the funny part. I remember how surprised he was when Roosevelt didn't get it, but he was always talking about Garner. How Garner would or wouldn't do this."

"That is strange," she said.

"Strange, but not very important. They were all the same: Garner, Baker, Roosevelt. When Baker got in, he did just what Tommy predicted: not a damn thing. People don't matter. Just events. History. Except for Tommy. He didn't sit back and let history happen; he went out and made it himself."

"I suppose he did," she said.

Ennis nodded, turned, and looked at the room as if seeing it for the first time. There were eight wooden tables, four chairs beside each one. Then came the jukebox, the polished linoleum floor, and the bar. Then Molly. There wasn't much to see.

"I'm going to bed," he said.

"I suppose so."

He got to his feet and tried to smile at her, but it was too late for that. Like the rest of him, his facial muscles were numb and dead. He said, "You've been good to me. I appreciate it, Molly."

"And tomorrow?" she asked.

"Who knows? I'll get out of here, that's for sure. I've caused you enough trouble. You listened to me and that was what I needed."

"Where will you go?"

"I'll find a place."

"I think I'll go to bed with you," she said, reaching across the bar.

"That would be nice," he said.

"I think so too." And she smiled again—the old way.

Chapter Six

The first time Rachel ever set eyes on Tommy Bloome was exactly two days before Christmas of that year. Which was rather fortunate, the date falling so near an easily remembered holiday because with her normally confused sense of time she might never have been able to remember it otherwise and that date was one she never wanted to forget. Of course, it was also exactly four weeks before they were married, and if she wanted to find the date, she could always subtract twenty-eight from their anniversary date, which she knew well since it was written down, and come up with an answer that way. December had thirty-one days, so that meant it had to be December 23, 1930. Yes, she remembered clearly now.

One of them at least must have been drunk. No, not Tommy, he was never drunk, she meant her and Billy. She was sure of that as soon as the funny waiter who reminded her of a gorilla dressed in a tux she had seen in a movie the week before finished showing them to their table. Any person of her position—or Billy's—wouldn't have been found dead in a rundown dive like this place. What was the horrid name? Wasn't it Tony's? No, it wasn't quite that horrid; it was Anthony's. Still, what a dreadful name for the dive. And the real problem was that she wasn't positive it was Billy who was drunk. That was William E. Sonderson III. For most of the past year Billy had been her devoted escort. She loathed him, such a nonentity, albeit he was descended from one of the most distinguished families in the East. A better family than her own, although, frankly, her father could have bought and sold a dozen Sondersons on the open market and managed to turn a profit. Billy's father, they said, had lost his shirt and underwear in the Big Crash. Her own father— brilliant, brilliant man—had sold out ahead of time, following the lead of several other smart operators, Kennedy and so on. The Sondersons, this was the rumor at least, had recently been forced to let go of two maids and a wrinkled butler, all three of whom dated clear back to the original Senator William Sonderson, who had fought the Versailles Treaty with Henry Cabot Lodge. But Rachel's money—well, her father's money, actually—was brand-new tainted money. Yet you could still spend it. That was the part that amused her. So what if her grandfather had started his adult years as a railroad conductor? And her grandfather's father had not even been that; he had been an Irishman. Her mother's family was decent and respectable but, because of that, seldom seen. Her mother had died giving birth (to Rachel) and, once her death was firmly established, the family had tended to forget her past existence. So Billy Sonderson still took the liberty of referring to her (in public too) as "my little green-eyed Irish waif."

But he only talked that way when he was drunk, like now.

It was no wonder she despised the brown-eyed, blue-blooded, little son of a bitch.

And here they were, together, two days before Christmas, in sweet San Francisco.

She had never been to California, so when Billy called and said, "I'm freezing, Rachel, and don't think I can bear another minute of this terrible winter. Why not let's you and I take a train to California where we can kiss Santa Claus under the sun?" She said, "Sure," confiding that she was, in fact, "already packed." She wasn't but with Father in Europe she might as well have been.

But, damn it, she really wished she could decide which of them was drunk because then she would also know which of them had suggested this dive. The bar was nearly hidden behind a pile of squat dark men in long overcoats. They were wearing their hats indoors too. The tables weren't so bad, but the floorshow was even worse, consisting of a bony blonde in a floor-length, skin-tight gown, gurgling away at some pathetic song about love. While Rachel drank and fidgeted, Billy drank and stared, acting like a twelve-year-old with a hard-on, trying to uncover the tips of the singer's barely concealed tits.

Rachel said, "Because you've got more money than anybody in this room doesn't mean she's going to pull up her dress and sit in your lap. One of those gangsters at the bar is probably her boyfriend and is apt to come over here and rub you out." She giggled. "That would be funny."

Billy didn't even glance at her. He acted as if he hadn't heard a single word. Well, that proved it. He was drunk, all right, the bastard.

It was cold in here. If Billy was sober, she'd have told him to get her coat. She was afraid to go herself. She had a feeling that if she stood up, one of those dark men would step up and politely rape her. They reminded her too much of that horrid Enrico who had sent them here in the first place. Oh. So that was how it happened. She remembered everything now. Billy had this painful habit of picking up with the weirdest, most desperate characters. She thought Enrico had carried a gun, though when she asked him he had said no.

"Well, what do you think?" Billy said, using a hand to sweep the length of the room. The girl had disappeared from the stage. "What about this place?"

"It makes me sick."

"Oh, yeah?" He raised an eyebrow. "Is that so?"

"That's what I said."

"You think—what?—you think it's beneath your dignity."

"Well, it's certainly not beneath yours."

"I thought you liked to live a little." He let his fingers creep across the tabletop and tried to grab her hand, but she slid easily free. "Your father can buy and sell my father. Don't tell me you've forgotten."

"I remember."

"You do? Oh, really? Rachel, I'm so glad. I can see that you're going to take your father's puny ten million and transform it into something truly worthwhile, a fit companion to the Malone name. You will be a true wizard of finance. I must phone New York and warn Morgan of your budding genius. If your father lets you have the money. Which isn't all that damn likely. Considering the way you carry on."

"He'll let me have it," she said, laughing, forgetting his presence momentarily. "Who else?"

"A fair question," Billy said. "But I was only joshing. I'm sure you'll get your slice. And you've got that bundle of your grandfather's money too. But how much of it is left, I wonder."

"That is none of your business."

"Right again." He was nodding slowly as if keeping time to music only he could hear. "So why don't we get the hell out of here? I've seen enough gangsters for one day. They all look the same in the movies."

"I'm ready," she said.

"You usually are. We'll have to go to bed when we get back."

"Talk to your skinny singer. I'm not interested."

"Rachel, Rachel," he said with mock sadness. "Since when? Last night, ah, last night—the train, tiny cramped berth. You had fun, right?"

"You were sober then."

"So? What's wrong with a drink now and then? Am I too wild for Rachel the pure?" Raising his glass, he leered at her, then drank, dribbling.

He was much drunker than she had thought. His eyes seemed unable to focus and his neck waggled as if his head were too heavy for it. He talked clearly, but that was typical. When Billy got drunk, he suddenly turned clever as a cat.

"You were a pain last night too," she said. "I've known prep-school boys who—"

"Oh, yeah?" he said loudly. "Is that what you like? Pale, hairless little boys."

"Dave, your brother. I wish he— What is he now? Fifteen? I wish you were him instead of you. I bet he could—"

"Oh, leave me alone." She had turned him sullen. "I've heard enough from you. Leave my brother alone."

"I didn't—"

"Liar! I said shut up!"

She could see it was no use. She tried to catch his hand. "Come on, Billy. Please. Let's go."

He said, "No," pouting. "I like it here. This is my kind of place."

"Then you can stay here and enjoy it," she said. "Alone." And she stood up.

"Ah, the hell with you." Sweeping out with one long arm, he neatly cleared the tabletop of its contents. Everything crashed to the floor: two tall glasses filled with liquor and ice, an unlabeled pint bottle of Scotch. The checked table-cloth dangled precariously from one corner of the table. Billy pointed at it and laughed.

Then his forehead snapped forward and smacked loudly against the bare tabletop. He moaned once, and Rachel felt ill.

The man who had sapped Billy—it was the gorilla-waiter—turned to the crowd and said, "You people, go back to what you were doing. This is nothing we can't handle."

Rachel stared at Billy. He was bleeding; she could actually see the blood.

The waiter looked down at her and smiled in a friendly way. "Who was he?"

For a second Rachel thought he meant Billy was dead. *Was,* he had said, but now she could hear him breathing; he sounded like an old man fast asleep, snoring.

"I never saw him before in my life," she said.

"He was drunk?"

"He wanted to lay me. I told him to go away."

"I thought you came in with him. I thought I saw—"

"He grabbed me just outside the door."

"You live in the city?"

"New York."

The waiter nodded as if this fact explained everything else. His teeth were ugly and yellow. "I'll take care of him for you," he said. "Is that O.K.?"

"Yes," she said, "that would be fine." Too many eyes were watching her; time to get away. She stood, stepped carefully past the spilled liquor and broken glass, and made her way toward the powder room.

The waiter called after her to promise that he would have the mess cleared away in no time at all. A nice, beautiful man.

Meanwhile, passing the tables, most packed with a couple or more, Rachel smiled; the tables smiled back. A few, the most polite, bent their knees and gave crisp little bows. Rachel was impressed. Such happy, friendly tables, she thought. Seldom met a table that will smile or bow. Must be the gorgeous California climate. Puts them in a good mood. Special kind of lumber. What is it? Redwood. Come to California, where there's ne'er a flake of snow. Who had told her that? Dumb

Billy. It hadn't stopped raining since they'd arrived. Bellboy said they should have gone to Los Angeles. Full of movie stars. Maybe a big producer would've discovered her. Maybe . . .

Passing through the powder-room door, she turned in time to catch a glimpse of the gorilla-waiter heading toward the back door with a big dark object under his arm. Billy, she realized. That was the dark object's name. She giggled.

But when she discovered the powder room presently uninhabited, she went quickly to the back and sat down on a bench and began to cry. Damn, damn, damn. It wasn't what had happened that made her cry so much as the fact that it had happened again. Not that all her escorts were in the habit of getting sapped in speakeasies. In New York it would never have happened because they would have known her and Billy. It was things: the way dumb, stupid, ugly things were always happening to her. She hadn't hurt anyone. What she wanted from life was a little bit of fun because it wasn't going to last forever. She was already old. All she wanted was a few more good times and yet here she was three thousand miles from home, sobbing into her hands like a pregnant debutante. Thinking only made it seem worse, but certain facts were true, and that helped. She tried to list them: her name was Rachel Constance Malone; her father's name was Daniel Malone; he was a millionaire sportsman and owned a twenty-eight-room house on Long Island; she was twenty-six years old; her father was fifty-nine; her mother was dead; in the streets of America, millions of hungry men went looking for work; in a back alley in San Francisco, a boy named Billy Sonderson lay bleeding in the rain; she, Rachel Malone, was so damn sick sick sick of it all.

When she emerged from the powder room, her cheeks and eyes were clean and white, stripped of any past despair. Another party had been seated at her table. She shrugged. It was time to go anyway. Maybe she ought to look out and see if Billy was gone. In any event, she had enough money to get back to the hotel and enough additional money in her room for a ticket to New York. That meant she would be spending Christmas Day on the train, but she refused to worry; she trusted Santa Claus to find her no matter where she was.

She started for the back door but stopped beside one table. She had not noticed the people—two men and a woman—before. They were poorly dressed, though not like gangsters, and one of the men had bright red hair. The waiter was talking to the redhead, saying loud enough so that Rachel could clearly hear, "I'm afraid you're going to have to go. Anthony's sorry, but . . . you know . . . some people . . ."

Rachel was delighted to find another person whose world was not a tight happy little sanctuary. She stood behind the waiter and laughed shrilly.

The waiter turned angrily.

"Excuse me," Rachel said, "but these people are with me."

The waiter, recognizing her, laughed. "Not these," he said.

"Sure, they are," said Rachel.

"No, we're not," said the redhead, but he was smiling.

"What's wrong with you?" Rachel asked. "Don't you smell good?"

"We throw bombs."

The waiter interrupted; he was no longer smiling. "That guy over there—see him?—his father owns the *Express*. He comes in here all the time, a bad apple, and he knows you, Tommy. He wanted to know what you were doing here, and I told him you were drinking, and he said maybe he'd better start going someplace else. So I asked Anthony and he said—"

"I get the picture," the redhead said. "The *Express*, huh?"

"Yeah, and it's a cruddy paper too."

"Sometimes I miss Hearst."

"Who?" asked the other man at the table.

"Nobody," the redhead murmured.

"There used to be a senator from California named Hearst. George Hearst, I think it was, but—"

"I said forget it," the redhead said. He got up, gesturing at the others to do likewise. Satisfied, the waiter wandered off.

Rachel didn't. "Is what he said about you true?" she asked.

"Every word," the redhead said.

"I'm Rachel Malone. Daniel Malone is my father."

"I'm Tommy Bloome. And this is Bob Ennis and Molly

Killian." They were walking toward the cloakroom. Rachel moved effortlessly along beside them.

"My father is a millionaire," she said.

"We're impressed," Bob Ennis said.

"No, we're not," said Tommy. "After the revolution you and your father will be as broke as any of us. Then it won't matter."

"What will happen to it?"

"Your father's money? Oh, we'll use it to buy Arab babies. I suppose you know Reds like to eat babies and the tastiest are the Arabs. Their blood makes a good wine too." He passed her a coat, which turned out to be hers, then a hat. His own coat was the shabby kind lumberjacks wear.

The other man drove. She rode in the back with Tommy Bloome. The car clanked up steep hills that seemed to rise and rise forever. She didn't mind. She had never met anyone like Tommy Bloome in her life: he wasn't afraid of her father. Not only that, but he claimed to believe in something —an idea, of all things—and she just had to find out more about that. In fact, if she hadn't been so drunk, she would probably have made him tell her all the ideas in which he believed, listing them carefully one by one so that she could believe in them herself.

"It's cold," she said unceremoniously, and she snuggled close against him.

"Is it?" he asked.

"Yes," she insisted.

"Are you sure?"

She snuggled closer. "Positive."

When they reached the storefront, Tommy had to argue with Bob Ennis. Molly Killian had disappeared someplace en route. She wished Ennis would go away too. He kept calling her "that damned rich tramp."

At last Ennis thudded up a flight of rickety stairs. Tommy said, "This way," and led her through the store—it was abandoned and empty—to a room behind where there were tiny wooden chairs fit for dwarfs and a big gray machine that stunk of oil and ink.

"I need a drink," she said, squeezing into one of the midget chairs.

"There's beer upstairs in the kitchen."

"Ugh."

"There's nothing else."

"I'll do without."

She noticed the cot now too. The mattress was brown with dirt, and if it wasn't full of bugs, then her name was Groucho Marx. If he wanted to lay her, he'd have to find a better place. She wasn't that drunk.

"I'm freezing," she said.

"We can only afford to heat this place for the meetings. You better keep your coat on."

"You have your meetings here?" She was amused. Was this the secret headquarters of that conspiracy dedicated to taking her father's money away from him? Fat chance. "I'll give you a check for a thousand dollars," she said, "then you can let me light the stove."

"A bribe?" he asked.

"Contribution."

"Thanks"—he shook his head—"but your father would stop the check and then we'd be out not only the cost of coal but also a thousand dollars besides."

She started to laugh at his joke, but he turned suddenly away, seated himself in one of the chairs, uncovered a type-writer from someplace in the clutter, and set it on a small table. He rolled a sheet of paper into the machine and began typing away. The paper was longer and wider than a normal sheet and was coated with a thin layer of blue film.

"What's that?" she asked, standing and crossing over.

"A mimeograph stencil," he said.

She watched him type. He had removed his shirt and rolled his shirtsleeves up past the elbows. His forearms were pale, slender, lightly freckled.

"What are you writing?"

"An incitement to riot."

"Not here?"

"On the docks. A strike. But we won't succeed. Not this time. Maybe next time."

"Will that be the revolution?"

"Only a strike. When all workers go on strike at the same moment, that will be the revolution. Or the start of it, any-way."

"Why?" she asked.

"Why do we do it?" She had got him to stop typing. "I could spend all night answering that."

"No, why are you so sure it's going to happen? It's never happened before. The Depression will be over by summer, and then that'll be it."

"No, it won't," he said. "I know your father told you that, but he's wrong. The Depression is going to last just long enough for everything to boil over and there's nothing your father can do to stop it. The fault is his anyway. He and all his friends, too, are so busy trying to save their own necks they can't see they're bringing down the whole system at the same time." Rachel felt a tiny rising thrill building deep down in her belly. She loved the fervor, passion, the dedication she heard in his tone. "If your father were right now to say 'All right, we know these aren't good times so what we're going to do is forgo all profits until the current situation is resolved. We have enough money as it is, so we're going to try to spread some of the excess around. Every man will receive double wages, nobody can work more than thirty hours a week, and we're going to increase our labor force by half to fill the gap.' Would it work? I don't know, but if all of them did something—I don't care what— I'd be out on the street inside a week, looking for something to occupy my time. And they would also be saving their own precious hides."

"My father would never do that."

"I know."

"So then, what are you going to do? Are you going to kill him?"

"Oh, no. We have something much worse in mind."

She laughed. "The only thing worse would be taking his money."

He laughed. "Now you've guessed it." He went back to the typewriter. *Clickety-clickety-click.*

"I have some money of my own," she said. "My grandfather left it to me when he died. If you were me, what would you do with it?"

He didn't answer. *Click-click-tap-click.* Past his shoulder she was able faintly to read the tiny alphabetical slices in the filmy skin of the stencil: ". . . necessary for an equitable sharing of national industrial wealth."

"Do dock workers really understand such big words?" she asked.

Stopping again, he tuned and said, smiling, "What makes you think we're writing for them? They know the truth; this is for their bosses to read. The men don't strike for abstract reasons. They do it because they've got kids at home who are hungry, because their brother's kids are starving. These men know they're lucky, they still have a job of sorts even if the bosses choose who works and turn around and pay pennies as wages, but they know others who aren't so lucky and it makes them think."

"It bothers them. How come?"

He shrugged, typing again. Rachel continued to read each new word as the keys engraved it upon the surface of the stencil. Her eyes began to water.

"How long are you going to be?"

"Not too long. I'll be through here in a minute, then we can run it off. A couple hours."

Clickety-clickety-clack-clack.

"Do you want me to help?"

"Do you know how to run a mimeograph?"

"No."

"I'll show you. Take off your coat. I hope you won't mind getting ink on you dress."

"Maybe I should take that off too." She gave him a lewd wink; she had seen it done in the movies.

"No, don't do that. It's cold in here, remember?"

She shivered for him delicately, then tried to pout. "You're mean to me."

"It's your money I wish to take, not your virgin body."

That made her laugh and laugh. Virgin indeed.

Tommy typed another line, stopped to read what he had written, then ripped the stencil free of the machine. "Come along," he said, passing the stencil to her.

Beside the mimeograph, he explained to her briefly how the machine functioned. Then, while she removed her coat, he got from a drawer what looked like a small tin of black paint. With a wide brush he painted the central cylinder of the machine with the thick, black, moist ink. The odor of the ink reminded her powerfully of rancid fish. She held her nose while Tommy fastened the stencil to the painted cylinder. Some of the ink squished around the edges, but he carefully wiped those places with a dry rag.

"Now," he said, "here's how it works, so listen to me this time because I'm not going to tell you again. The stencil is full of holes where the typewriter cut out the letters. When you turn the handle here, it turns the cylinder and also forces the paper into the machine between the cylinder and the rubber roller below. The ink comes through the holes in the stencil as the cylinder turns. This causes the letters to be printed on the paper. When you're done, the paper will come out the opposite end onto the tray. If you've done it right, the text ought to be printed neatly on the page. You have to turn the crank at the right speed, though, or else the ink will be too light or heavy. Think you can manage it?"

"Sure. I turn the handle. That's all."

"Yes. And insert the paper. Slide it forward till it catches between the cylinder and the roller. That part's easy after a while and you won't even have to think about it."

"Sure."

"Now go get a handful of paper. Over there."

For the first few pages, Tommy turned the handle, instructing her on how to feed the paper at the proper moment so that the text was evenly printed upon the finished page. Then she tried herself and squealed with delight as the page emerged from the machine. But it was unreadable; the ink had smeared. "Crank faster," Tommy said. "Then, when it starts getting lighter, slow down."

She did it that way and the page turned out all right.

"Go to town," he said, "but remember to check each page when it comes from the machine. When the ink gets to be too faint no matter how slow you're cranking, call me and I'll paint the cylinder again."

"O.K."

Tommy went over and sat down. With nimble dancing fingers he rolled a cigarette faster than her eyes could follow. He struck a match against the chair leg and flipped the burned stick over his shoulder when done.

Rachel didn't dare stop to watch him. She continued to crank the handle. First page, turn, second page, turn, look, third page, turn. Already her hands were covered with ink.

She wiped them against the hem of her gown and cranked some more.

"This is fun," she said after fifteen successful cranks. "I haven't been this sober in a month." Page sixteen. "How many did you say you need?"

"Oh, two or three hundred. I'll let you know when to quit."

She groaned at him.

After the first hundred copies, Tommy came and applied a second coat of ink. By now Rachel's arm was so sore she could hardly move it, but she deliberately kept the injury from Tommy. There was enough ink on her body and dress to fill an inkwell twice over, but she didn't mind that either.

"Go to it," Tommy said, latching the stencil onto the cylinder. "You're getting there." He went back to his chair, sat down, rolled a cigarette. "Still cold?"

"Cold?" She laughed, cranking. "I'm sweating like a scrubwoman."

"Why do you wear your hair like that?"

"You mean cut short? Bobbed?"

"Wouldn't it look better long? Around your shoulders at least. This is 1930, you know. There's a depression on. The Jazz Age is over. F. Scott Fitzgerald is dead."

"Is he?"

"His world is."

"I read a story by him once. A couple of them, but only one I remember." She cranked and cranked, the revolving drum growing hazy beneath her eyes. Pain crept from her wrist to her elbow to her biceps to her shoulder. Ouch. Her whole right side ached like the devil in hell. "The story was about people like you, about communists. They were doing some printing in an office and these men—they were veterans of the war—broke in and beat them up and threw some out the windows. Is that what's going to happen to us?"

One hundred twenty copies.

"There aren't any windows in here."

"Have you ever been beaten?"

"Many times."

"Tell me about one time."

He told her about a ranch in the Central Valley where he had tried to start a strike, only the strike had failed and the men, blaming him, had gone and told their bosses, who had sent goons to beat him and then throw him in a ditch. "There weren't any windows out there either," he said.

Having him talk made the work proceed much faster for Rachel. She even lost count of the number of pages and finally, after struggling to remember, confessed to him. He said, "That's O.K.—I think we've got enough. Run a few more till the ink starts to fade, then we'll quit."

When she finished, he came and removed the wet stencil from the machine. He slipped it inside a drawer along with many other used stencils. "Next year," he said, "when the same thing happens again, we'll be ready."

Then he switched off the light and led her to the stairs, then up the stairs. At the top they followed a long hallway and passed many rooms on both sides, all of which seemed to be presently in use, filled with a minimum of three sleeping bodies.

At the end of the hallway was a bathroom with a sink.

"I don't know if you'll be able to get any hot water this late, but maybe you can get rid of some of the ink. Try not to dirty more than one towel."

When he was gone, she shut the door—it wouldn't lock—then removed her dress and tossed it carelessly behind the toilet. Standing shoeless in her slip, she scrubbed her face and hands with soap and cold water. Then she sat on the edge of the tub and rolled down her stockings. Standing again, she looked into the mirror and wondered if that funny, scrubbed, smeared face was really her own. What would Daddy think?

She opened the door and Tommy was there.

He took her elbow.

Their room—to her relief—turned out to be otherwise unoccupied. The bed itself was clean; the sheets were white, stiff, new. She took off her slip. Tommy turned out the lights.

Four weeks later, after a bitter visit with her father during which he had informed her she would never see another of his nickels and she had told him there wouldn't be any more nickels after the revolution, Rachel Malone married Tommy Bloome. They spent their honeymoon in Hollywood, which turned out to be a bourgeois bore, then settled in a three-room apartment on Bush Street downtown.

In the Hollywood hotel, their first married night, she failed to come; with him, she always had before. She faked it though, and assumed she was tired.

"Are you glad?" she asked him.

"Yes," he said, lying wet and spent and naked beneath her. "Aren't you?"

"In a way—and I don't mean this wrongly—I haven't sobered up since that first night."

"Me either," he said, yawning.

"But aren't you glad?"

"I said I was."

"But are you sure?"

"Yep."

"Me too." Then she kissed him. "I really am," she said.

Chapter Seven

As the years passed—1931 becoming 1932 and then 1933 and finally, already, it was 1934—her existence seemed to alternate as his attentions wavered, swaying regularly back and forth like a clock's pendulum, between the tick and the tock, the in and the out, the white and the black. Not only separate, but opposing. The first time she really understood that this was fated to be was late in '32, when Tommy abruptly disappeared for two months and she never heard a word except a brief note from New York saying he was fine and hoping she was fine too. Only later did she guess that he must have gone to Europe (and probably to Moscow) because, shortly after his return to Bush Street, he presented her with a perfectly charming Swiss timepiece and also a silver bracelet plainly made in Russia. It was right after that that he said, "We're going to have to give up this place."

"Our home?"

"We're moving to New York. I'm a deputy secretary now."

"But"—she pointed to yesterday's copy of the party newspaper published in New York which she reviewed religiously in hopes of spying some vague mention of Tommy Bloome —"I didn't see it."

He grinned. "A secret."

"But—not New York."

"You have friends there."

"Oh, but, Tommy, that was such a long time ago."

"Two years?"

She hated it. New York. Afraid even to venture beyond the casual boundaries of her neighborhood. Tommy had bought a nice home in a decent section of Brooklyn—that was safe. But anywhere else, there was always the risk:

what if she met one of her old friends? What would they say? How would they treat her? She didn't want to go through that for anything.

But sometimes she had to go out, and when she went (not always, no, but it seemed like always), they were waiting for her, watching, staring. They never spoke to her nor she to them, but she could see their lips moving, tongues flapping, and she heard, always heard:

"There goes Rachel Malone. Thirty years old now. Still pretty—yes, in a way—but look, look at the way she's dressed. Good God! Where could she ever have found that —that sack. A garbage pail, a garbage pail in Brooklyn, if you can believe that. She lives there with that man. A long article about him yesterday in the *Times*. The most dangerous man in America, they say, but I wouldn't give him a second glance except for her. She was mentioned, of course. Old Mr. Malone won't allow her name mentioned in his presence. Does he have a servant censor the papers before reading them? I'm sick of him myself. He's ugly. Skinny as a stick. Red hair too. And Irish. They claim he paid the man who tried to shoot the President. The foreigner in Florida, he was one of them too. But why bother with Baker? I almost miss Hoover. Arthur tells me there's a standing offer in the club—a joke, so don't tell anyone—a million dollars cash to the man who shoots Bloome. Don't tempt me, I told him. I wonder if Rachel has heard. She might want to do it for less than a million. From the looks of that sack twenty dollars might be enough. I'll tell Arthur. Why doesn't he feed her? Spend some of that Moscow gold on his wife. Is he a Jew? Do they have children? I don't think she can. I think she's damaged. When she used to get drunk, she'd tell you anything. What she did with men. She must have caught a disease, the things she'd do. Tom Daley the lawyer taught her. He made her do almost anything and she never hesitated to tell. It made me ill. If Arthur even suggested to me, I think I'd kill him. Well, she got what she deserved. She'll never have his child."

She wasn't damaged, but there hadn't been time for children. And now it was 1934 and that was the time of revolution.

For Rachel Bloome the months of the Second American

Revolution were a time of darkness. And light, too—bright, harsh, glaring, endlessly flickering neon light. Hotel rooms. One after the other. As many as five and six and seven in a single week. She saw Tommy infrequently, as if by accident. He would enter her room, talk, then leave. Or else she would meet him in some half-lighted basement rendezvous deep in the city slums. Chicago one week, Detroit, then way westward to Oakland, Calif. Never the same city two weeks in a row. She and Tommy were both running, but their paths seldom converged. After the successes of July she often heard him on the radio; his photograph appeared daily in the loyal press. They called it a revolution, wanting to justify their treason with visions of Washington, Jefferson, and Patrick Henry. But it was just war, Rachel understood that all along.

It commenced with the general strike of February 18, 1934, and continued through the first sporadic fighting in March and April. Tommy was indicted for treason at the end of that month. The farmers' revolt culminated immediately thereafter and food supplies dwindled, then vanished. Newton Baker resigned May 3; his successor died less than two weeks later—"heart attack" said the few newspapers able to publish. The cities exploded in flames. There was no new President; instead, the cold clenched steel fist of martial law slammed down upon the American nation. Honest war erupted; casualties mounted. In July the army revolted against its officers and Tommy Bloome, from his secret headquarters, proclaimed the establishment of the Free Democracy of the United States of America. Not that the fighting ceased; in fact, it grew more fierce, for now the generals were fighting for their very lives. Tens of thousands died during those few months of autumn. Nationalist and Red. Soldier and civilian. For a time it seemed as though the fighting would not end until all of America lay dead. It did end. By November it was as good as over and the new constitution was published. Joseph Stalin telegrammed his personal congratulations and promised immediate recognition; however, the Soviet ambassador failed to reach Denver until March, by which time the capital had been returned to Washington and nineteen additional countries had recognized the new regime. Hitler never did, or Italy until after Mussolini's disappearance. It was also in March when the last of the Nationalist generals—Douglas MacArthur himself—reached Canada. At the end of the month, Britain agreed to withdraw the troops belatedly sent streaming across the border in December, 1934. Under the terms of an amnesty the Nationalist troops were dispersed from their last strongholds. The remnants who rejected surrender took refuge in the Colorado Rockies and were eventually hunted down and killed by local constables; by then, these proud soldiers had become mere petty thieves.

For a year she ran. Bob Ennis, her only companion. She never quite understood why they (the army, police, whoever) wanted to find her so desperately; what she knew of Tommy was nothing. Maybe Ennis knew, but it wasn't him they were chasing. Before dawn he would wake her and they would run down the battered back stairs of the cheap New Orleans hotel and into the half-lighted street below, where an idling car was waiting to rush them away to some new but not different hideaway. A change of wigs. Perhaps blonde this time. Then the train. Ennis in a beard and moustache. Dallas, this time. A cheap hotel. And maybe—just maybe and not very often—Tommy would be waiting.

"You're all right?"

"Yes—yes, I suppose so."

"That was close back there."

"I know."

"We're better situated here."

"If they catch me?"

"Do you want me to lie?"

"Why bother?"

"They'll shoot you."

"I don't know anything."

"What do you need?"

"Nothing."

A pause. The only one he ever permitted himself. Then, "This won't last forever, Rachel, I want you to remember that."

"I will. But him"—pointing at Ennis, who never left her sight whether Tommy was present or not—"does he have to be here all the time?"

"I trust him."

But he never understood.

After July her circumstances should have got better, but she was in Boston when the army revolt occurred and the Nationalists maintained firm control of the eastern cities. Train service west was shut down, which meant she was trapped, stuck. She continued moving from city to city and hotel to hotel, but within a more limited range now. The main change was that she started sleeping during the day; at night the fighting outside was too noisy. In Newark one night Tommy's own men burned down the hotel in which she was staying. Funny. She and Ennis were forced to spend the night with the other refugees in a city park. That was in August. She fell asleep easily in the relative coolness of the park.

Three days later in New Haven she attempted to seduce Bob Ennis. Funny. She didn't dare wait till night, knowing she'd lose her nerve when the shooting started, and they were alone now. She hadn't slept with Tommy or any man since February, but that wasn't why she acted. It was Ennis himself. After living with him for half a year, she was curious to see him—once, just once—responding like a real man and not a robot, a cold inhuman calculating machine. But he would not, maybe he could not. He slipped easily out of her clutches, making no effort to conceal his contempt. She said he was a fairy and knew it. He laughed. Then she said he was a fairy for Tommy and he said, "I'm a friend of Tommy's. That's something you'll never be able to understand."

This same day—actually, the night—was also notable because Rachel started drinking again. She had not touched an other-than-social drop since the day she had married Tommy Bloome. Even during the depths of Brooklyn she had remained stone sober, but this night she decided to get bombed like an angel and, falling asleep, passing out, slept in a warm and dreamless haze. After that, she never went anywhere without her bottle. When Ennis was near, she would cuddle the bottle close to her chest as if it were a doll and sing snatches of half-forgotten lullabies while rocking rhythmically from side to side. She kissed the bottle, licked the stem with her tongue, waved it like a battle flag. "Drink, Ennis!" she cried. "Get smashed. Enjoy life for a change."

He always refused politely.

In October Tommy was shot. Ennis came and told her and added that she would be permitted to visit him for a few days. Strangely they encountered no difficulties reaching the waiting plane, a fat converted bomber decorated with blazing red stars. The plane hopped from Boston to Chicago to Denver. A boring ride. Below, large chunks of the American continent—fields and mountains and rivers and lakes—rolled past in blinding, blurring procession. Everybody, even the pilot of the plane, had to tell her about Tommy. He wasn't hurt. The wound was superficial. The pilot, who remarkably resembled John Gilbert with a moustache, claimed he'd actually seen Tommy. "And he's doing splendidly, Mrs. Bloome, absolutely."

"Then why put me through this ordeal?" she asked.

Ennis said, "Shut up." Rachel was drunk and he made it a point to avoid conversing with her when she was. Funny. That meant they seldom exchanged more than a half-dozen phrases first thing upon rising—from separate beds, of course.

Rachel didn't want to talk to him anyway.

This morning he had been full of morbid news regarding the assassination attempt. While he talked, she searched the room in hopes of finding some remainder of last night's bottle. Ah, she found it, eventually, hidden under the bed, nasty little thing, good sweet gin. She gulped and gurgled while Ennis informed her a fanatic had managed to penetrate Tommy's personal guard and fire a single bad shot before having his gun taken away and the barrel rammed up his butt. Tommy had suffered a minor flesh wound across his right forearm. Ennis insisted it was nothing serious.

"What about the other fellow?" Rachel asked.

"What other fellow?"

"The little guy."

"Oh, the assassin." Ennis pretended to hesitate, then eagerly divulged that it hadn't been pretty. No, sir. Tore him limb from limb, chunks carried back to the barracks as souvenirs suitable for stuffing.

"Is that why I have to go out there? To pose for simpering pictures with Tommy? He won't want me anyway when he learns how drunk I am. Tell him to go lead his army."

But when the car arrived to carry them to the airfield, she had gone willingly.

By the time the plane touched ground in Denver, Rachel
was sober. Well, almost sober. Ennis had to help her to the
waiting staff car. A bunch of red-starred army officers filled
the front seat, but Rachel and Ennis had the rear all to themselves. The scrubbed upholstery smelled like horses. Her father had raised them once, while he was still alive, and it was
an odor she'd never forget.

Her head ached. They were taking her to Tommy, she
kept telling herself, but that was not good medicine. The
remnants of the city of Denver were quickly left behind.
The unpaved road, pitted with the marks of war, ran through
hot, jagged country. It could have been hell out there. Everything was a big red rock. She shut her eyes, leaned against
the back of the seat, smelled horses, tried to forget.

When they reached the camp, they were eager to take her
directly to Tommy. She said no; she wanted to freshen up
first. She was promised the use of the officers' lounge. Ennis
accompanied her inside. She washed, using cold spring water
from wooden buckets, scrubbing her face more carefully than
in months. She applied fresh lipstick to her swollen mouth. She
rubbed the wrinkles and creases that highlighted her eyes,
nose, and lips, but they didn't go away that easily. She combed
her hair.

"I'm ready," she told Ennis.

"I sure as hell hope so."

A two-star general—the first clean uniform she had seen—
met them at the door.

"Where have you got my husband hidden?" she demanded
to know.

The general apparently knew about her. "This way, Mrs.
Bloome," he said sadly.

This way turned out to be another limousine. The hospital
was ten minutes from the main encampment. She saw mud
everywhere, some tents, and a lot of half-dressed men who
stopped whatever they were doing—usually nothing much—
and saluted the passing car. She waved back, giggling at
them.

Ennis misunderstood. "The fighting has lessened near here.
The main Nationalist army has retreated farther south. Their
bombers hit us two or three times a week, but they have only
a few planes left."

As soon as she stepped from the limousine, she realized this was going to be a mess. Anything, she thought, but not them: reporters. At least this bunch was polite; they let her proceed into the hospital tent and even stood back to let her pass. But, as soon as she was safely inside, they followed, cameras suddenly exploding against her back. She flinched beneath the bright assault and stepped quickly. A doctor grabbed her hand—white jacket, blood-stained. He spoke furiously, waving long hands, and it was some time before she understood he was saying Tommy would survive the monstrous, brutal, savage attack on his life.

"Yeah, I know." She had never wanted a drink this bad in her life. Hell, she could taste that sweet gin already. "Where've you got him hidden?"

"Hidden? But, Mrs.—"

"Take us to Tommy," Ennis said, intervening hastily.

"Oh, yes. Of course. This way, please."

As they moved into the darker recesses of the tent, Rachel avoided looking at the cots they passed. None seemed empty, and the odor of blood—she knew it at once—hung heavily in the stale air. And the rot, too. She was reminded of a slaughterhouse, though she had never seen one, not even in the movies. This was what one must be like, she was convinced. Animals—whether men or cattle—dead and dying, bleeding and rotting. She felt ill. A drink, a drink.

"Our most serious cases are taken immediately into the city hospitals where special care is available." This was the doctor, expounding. "These men you see here are all doing splendidly. Absolutely. We'll have them up and out and in the field in a matter of days."

A slaughterhouse, yes.

Tommy's bed wasn't any different from those which contained the other men. He seemed more slender than she remembered; his hair was brighter too. He was sitting up in bed, back braced against a fat pillow, the bedcovers rising to the lowest level of his ribcage. His wounded arm rested nakedly in his lap, a forgotten appendage, pale and sickly white, the bandage running from the wrist clear to the elbow. No blood was visible.

What else? She sighed, neither having spoken. The reporters formed a silent, expectant circle around the bed. One bumped her—accidentally—and she nearly fell across Tommy's arm. She held her mouth to keep from laughing. Joining her inside the circle were Ennis and the general and another man—thin with a broken nose—whom she had never seen before. Leaning over, he whispered something into Tommy's ear. The man didn't have a uniform but was dressed neatly in a black suit. Tommy grinned at whatever he had been told and jerked his head twice in agreement.

Then the tent exploded. Just cameras. Lights burst and flared. Rachel tried to smile but couldn't keep her gaze fixed to Tommy. Many primitive people believed the camera to be a device of the devil, capable of stealing a person's soul and locking it away. The unending flashes burned her eyes. Finally she couldn't look anymore.

When she opened her eyes, she couldn't see anything but a mess of bright blazing dots. They ran flickering through the air.

"How are you, Tommy?" she finally said.

"Just great, Rachel. I expect to be out of here tomorrow."

"I'm really glad to hear that, Tommy." Then, in another voice, one that seemed more truly her own, "The fellow who shot you is dead."

Tommy plainly struggled to conceal his irritation. "I know that, Rachel."

"Who's he?" She pointed at the thin man's broken nose. "This is John Durgas, my officer-in-charge."

A suspicion suddenly struck her. "He killed that little man."

"Rachel, don't be absurd."

"I'm sorry." She shrugged. "It was just a thought. She needed something else to say. But—what? The hospital was as still as the dead. The reporters shifted on silent feet. A light breeze had risen from somewhere and tickled her nose with its promise of outside freshness.

"Does it hurt?" she asked.

"Of course it does." Tommy was angry. No, now he was smiling. "I'm going to be fine now."

"Because he"—she found the doctor and pointed at him—"fixed you up?"

"No," Tommy said. "Because now you're here."

"Well, I would have come sooner."

"And I wish you could have." He smiled in sympathy, then started to laugh, but had to stop, moaning. "The doctor says I shouldn't do that," he explained. "Laughing is bad for me. I don't know why—I was shot in the arm."

She waved a hand at the circle of reporters. "Tommy, I can't get used to this."

"You'll have to learn. You're the most important woman in America, Rachel, you're the new first lady."

"Is Mrs. Baker dead?"

"No, she's all right. All of them are O.K."

"Oh."

"You are my wife, Rachel."

"I know that."

"It means you're the first lady."

"Does it?"

"Yes."

"Oh." She glanced hastily around, needing something, anything, to which she could briefly cling for support. Ennis stood rigidly at her elbow. She grabbed him, as if making an act of discovery. "Look, Tommy, here's Bob."

"I see. He's done a really fine job."

"Thank you, Tommy," said Ennis. Like Tommy, Ennis spoke directly at the reporters. Rachel was an observer here, not a participant. It was like a radio show. "We were never more than a step or two ahead of them," Ennis confirmed.

"Tell us more," Tommy said, his words acting as a signal. The reporters broke their circle, crowding around Ennis. Rachel could not see him anymore. A voice emerged from the mad cluster, apparently aimed at her, "Are you happy to be here?"

"Very happy," she said, mechanically. "It's like waking up from a long nightmare."

"You were nearly captured several times." The reporters had deserted Ennis. Now it was Rachel who was trapped at the center of their attentions. "What can you tell us about that, Mrs. Bloome?"

"It was bad."

"Where?"

"Oh, everywhere. I remember one time in New Orleans. Newark too, I think. Something happened there."

"Could you give us the details, please?"

"No."

"What?"

"I mean, I don't remember anything. The cities all blend together. I—" She searched for Tommy, needing help, but his bed was hidden behind a mass of notepads, cameras, and frowning men.

"But your escape today?"

"Oh, that was nothing either."

"What?"

It was Ennis who rescued her. Dear Bob. "The Nationalists are losing control in Boston. They have the regular police, their own troops, but the people are solidly with us. We took the Boston airfield away from them without any trouble. We kept it long enough to bring in a plane and get Mrs. Bloome off the ground. Then we let them have it back. Why risk the unnecessary loss of life? When the revolution is over, it'll be ours in the end."

"You didn't lose any men at all?" This voice carried a thick British accent. For the first time Rachel realized these reporters must be foreigners. She noticed several Japanese.

"Not on our side, no."

"Theirs?"

Ennis grinned. "We did all right. If you want a figure, ask them."

"And land in jail?" asked a reporter.

Everyone laughed at this. Rachel too. She took advantage of the pause to find Tommy again. He didn't seem to recognize her.

"Will you be staying in Denver permanently now, Mrs. Bloome?"

"I—" She looked at Ennis, who nodded down at Tommy.

"I don't think we should discuss that," Tommy said. "You gentlemen surely understand the need for secrecy."

"Of course."

"So are there any further questions?"

There were a few, all directed at Tommy. What will be your policy toward amnesty? Is it true Stalin has agreed to sell you aircraft? What about the Germans? Do you expect to have to send regular troops into the east? Tommy answered some questions, skillfully avoided others. Rachel, bored, listened with half an ear.

"After the war," said one man, "are you willing to accept a coalition form of government?"

"Why? We're winning. Coalitions are for losers."

The thin man, John Durgas, suddenly leaned over and whispered into Tommy's ear, shielding the movement of his lips with a cupped hand.

Then Tommy said, "I'm afraid Mrs. Bloome has had a difficult journey today. I think we should give her time to rest."

The reporters murmured to one another, as if they were discussing the situation. Ennis took Rachel by the elbow and, so fast she hardly knew what was happening, steered her toward the outside. She did turn and look back one time, but Tommy was already hidden from view.

They were passing the beds of blood and rot once more. She still didn't want to look.

"Oh, God, I need a drink," she said. "I need it now."

"No," said Ennis.

Chapter Eight

When the doctor returned from escorting the reporters out-side, Tommy Bloome rolled easily out of bed. "They're gone?"

"Yes, sir," the doctor said.

Tommy flexed his arm, clenching the fist and raising the knuckles to his shoulder. He lowered the hand, then raised it again. "A little stiff."

"Well, that was a bad wound, sir."

"I'll take care of it. I'll avoid hand-to-hand combat." Tommy looked at John Durgas, who stood beside the doc-tor. "Right, John?"

"You'll be fine," Durgas said.

Tommy told the doctor, "Have some pain-killers—pills, I guess—sent over to my tent. Now where did you hide my pants."

"But, sir—"

"But nothing. Go get them."

"Yes, sir."

Tommy chuckled as the doctor scurried away.

Durgas said, "Are you going to go see her?"

"I think I'd better talk to Ennis first."

"Yes, that would be best."

The doctor returned and, failing to conceal his disapproval, helped Tommy dress.

The doctor stepped away and said coldly, "Anything else you desire, sir?"

"Only those pills."

"Yes, sir."

"And I'll see you later, John. In my tent."

"Of course."

On his way out, Tommy paused and spoke to several of the wounded men. He told them they were doing fine. The fighting was nearly over now, and when it was, everyone was going to go home. He reiterated his promise of a good job for every soldier after the war was concluded. Ennis was waiting for him beside the tent flap. They fell into step.

"How's the arm?" said Ennis.

"Stiff at the edges. The guy was a crackpot. He tried to pot me at twenty yards with a .22 pistol. Lucky he got me at all. A fluke. Where's Rachel?"

"Staff headquarters. I had a colonel ousted to make room for her. I hope he wasn't anyone important."

"Not if he's only a colonel. Sometimes I think we have more generals in this army than privates."

"Is John Durgas a general?"

Tommy laughed. "I really haven't asked him."

They circled the hospital tent, finding a limousine parked there. The two men sat in the back seat and Tommy ordered the driver to take them to his tent.

"Yes, sir."

As the car rolled cautiously through the muddy camp streets, Tommy looked out the window, smiling to himself. Finally he turned to Ennis and asked, "What was the reaction to the shooting back east?"

"About what you'd expect. Sympathizers were shocked, neutralists were surprised, enemies were disappointed because he missed."

"And yourself?"

"I wondered why they didn't send a better man. If they were willing for you to become a martyr, they should have at least made sure you were a dead one."

Tommy grinned. "You were always smart, Bob."

"He wasn't a Nationalist agent."

"Nope. A nut. A private in one of our supply companies. Uncommitted. Came over with his division after the mutiny."

"Why'd he try to kill you?"

"They say because of his family. The father owned a little grocery store in Tucson. There was a bad food shortage down there about a month ago and the family tried hoarding. They were caught, tried, hanged by the revolutionary council. Father, mother, couple sisters. Of course, he blamed me."

"The Nationalists didn't know that. Their papers didn't even mention the attempt."

"But the people knew?"

"Sure."

"And they knew our version. That's why we're going to win this thing, Bob. The military mind lacks imagination. If it was me, I'd have issued a statement—and stuck it on the front pages of all my papers—saying a liberty-loving soldier had chosen to offer his life for the cause of freedom. Doomed but glorious attempt to strike down the tyrant Bloome. But they lost their chance; they didn't say a thing. So now history will accept our version, lie or not."

"You're becoming a regular Machiavelli, you know."

"I try. I've had to learn."

"Did Durgas teach you?"

"What makes you think so?"

"I've heard a lot about him."

"He's a good man."

"That's what I heard."

The car turned off the main road and plunged through a narrow ditch, spraying mud and water. Then, bouncing free of the ditch, it cut across a wide grassy field, devising a road of its own making.

"What are you going to do now?" Ennis said. "Do we stay or not? Was it only Rachel's picture you wanted or is there more to it than that?"

"I wanted to see her. You too, for that matter. I've kept you back east because it's really been the safest place in the country. Now I don't know, it's damn well over."

"Really? Or are you trying to feed me propaganda?"

"No, they're broke. They can't pay their troops, hardly even feed them. Their desertion rate is running several hundred a day. We've got them beat."

"It's been so easy."

"The hard part comes next."

"I know that."

"And I'll tell you the truth, I'm not looking forward to it. Revolution is easier than government. Now it'll be us that get blamed for everything wrong. But what about Rachel?"

"She's bad."

"Her father?"

"That part of it. I think you ought to talk to her."

"I plan to. Later. Tonight."

The car halted in front of an isolated tent. There was nothing but green grass for yards around the tent, not even a tree. Two soldiers, standing stiffly upright, flanked the entrance. Two additional men marched around the tent in opposing directions.

The tent was big enough so that both men could comfortably stand. A small cot and a wooden table occupied the dirt floor. Two duffel bags leaned against the cot and a gas lantern, hanging from the roof, cast a dull glow.

Tommy unfastened one of the duffel bags and, reaching inside, emerged with an unlabeled quart bottle.

"This is real bourbon," he said. "I think you'll find some cups in the corner. We'll sit here on the bed and talk and drink and get plastered."

Ennis brought the cups and Tommy filled them. They drank. Ennis seemed uneasy; he couldn't relax.

"What's wrong?" Tommy asked.

"Just Rachel, I guess. I've been around her too long. She doesn't like to be alone, so I worry."

"You think I should see her now?"

"I think you ought to."

"Maybe you ought to let me take care of my own wife."

"Whatever you say, Tommy."

Raising his cup, Tommy smiled. "Drink with me," he said. Ennis raised his cup and waited.

"To victory," Tommy said.

"To victory."

Tommy didn't get away till almost midnight. He wasn't drunk but maybe he wasn't entirely sober either. A sober man would have had the good sense to take a car, but here he was trying to walk the whole distance. From his tent to staff headquarters. What was it? To a flying crow, maybe a mile and a quarter. On these winding, muddy paths, twice that much at least. He wasn't tired. Hell, this little jaunt was nothing compared to some of the walks he had taken. The mud was a pain; his boots were filled with water. The chilled air froze his breath the instant it escaped his lips and nostrils. Above, the sky was clear and pure; directly overhead a big chunk of yellow moon squatted nakedly. The night, the moon, the liquor, the good talk with Ennis—he felt relaxed, almost mellow. He hadn't felt so good since that day in February when he'd received news that the New York police had decided to open fire on a picket line; twelve men had died. That was the first real spark. What was happening out in the country wasn't important, but New York was. Ten years of anticipation had ended for Tommy Bloome that day. The action of a single moment, a cop squeezing the trigger of his gun, and Tommy had known he had won, beaten history, vanquished time. And he was happy now too.

Ahead, abruptly, there was light. Tommy slowed his pace. Here was staff headquarters already. Six months ago this had been a plush winter resort, the main building a three-story hotel patterned after the design of an Alpine lodge, and to the left and behind the main building several smaller log cabins for long-term guests. The Nationalists had burned down most of the cabins when retreating, but they had for some reason chosen to leave the main hotel untouched. Tommy had turned the building over to his staff. Now it was filled with generals instead of millionaires, colonels instead of butlers. He preferred the austere privacy of a tent himself but never insisted his chief officers suffer with him.

A lone guard stood poised upon the porch. When Tommy approached, the soldier raised his rifle and called out.

"I'm Bloome," Tommy answered, striding into the light.

As soon as he saw Tommy, the guard snapped his rifle down, cracked his heels together, and saluted smartly.

"Don't do that to me," Tommy said. "I'm a civilian." He went on into the building.

This had been the lobby of the original hotel. A long desk still occupied the whole of one wall. A captain and sergeant were waiting here. At several small tables throughout the lobby various officers sat, playing cards, drinking, just talking. Tommy's entrance had immediately silenced the buzz of conversation. He went straight to the registration desk. The captain rushed forward, clutching a key in his fist. The sergeant didn't move from his place behind the desk; he rustled a few papers at Tommy.

"I have the key right here, sir," the captain said.

"That won't be necessary. Is she there?"

"I can send my sergeant to check."

"Her room number?"

"Fourteen, sir. You follow the corridor at the end of the lobby."

"I'll find it." He moved away, allowing the corridor to swallow him up. Out of sight of the lobby he paused and listened, hearing the sudden snap of a turned card, the tinkle of ice in a glass, the sound of relieved laughter. This was a sensation he still frankly enjoyed: that sense of absolute power. By simply walking into a room he could silence that room. Men he had never met in his life feared him for the sole reason that he was who he was, Tommy Bloome. It wasn't a feeling he enjoyed enjoying; it was like a perverse form of sex in that. There was something soiled and dirty about his reaction, but he could not help himself.

Room 14 was easily found. It sat forlornly at the dead end of the corridor. A streak of yellow light peeped from under the door.

Tommy knocked.

No answer.

He waited, then knocked again. "Rachel!"

The door opened and she was suddenly there.

He had intended to kiss and hold her. She met his gaze without flinching. "May I come in?" he asked.

"Sure, Tommy."

She stepped out of his way and allowed him to enter. Her room was larger than most. A door led into a private bath. A suitcase was open on the bed. He took a chair, sat down, looked up at her. She was dressed in a light frilly nightgown and matching slippers. Her eyes seemed strangely tired, almost aged.

He unlaced his boots, then slipped them off. He removed his socks. "Do you have a towel?"

She moved for the first time since he'd entered. "I can get you one."

While she was on her way to the bathroom, Tommy went over and draped his socks across the radiator. Rachel came back and handed him a towel. He dried his hands, went back to the chair, sat down, and wiped his feet.

"Why did you walk?" she asked, standing over him, eyes regarding his bare feet with open curiosity.

"I was drunk."

"You?" She laughed. "What time is it?"

He spread the towel on the floor and set his feet down upon it. "One, one-thirty."

"How did you know I wouldn't be asleep? Didn't Ennis tell you I've turned into a drunk."

"You don't look drunk."

"That's because I quit."

"When did you do that?"

"When I saw you today. I didn't see any more reason to drink."

"I'm glad," he said.

"You liar."

"Rachel, don't."

"Isn't that why you brought me here?"

"No. Sit down. I brought you here because I wanted to see you."

"Well, that isn't why I came. I wanted to see if that assassin was real."

"I can show you the wound."

"No, there's another reason too. I wanted to ask you one question."

"You can ask it now."

"Good." She sat down on the bed and crossed her legs. "Is it about your father?" he asked.

"I know all about him."

"What do you know?"

"I know you murdered him."

"Rachel, that's not true." He needed a drink badly. Damn it, this wasn't what he'd wanted. Why did she have to—

"Your people killed him."

"I can't control the actions of every mob in America. And I don't. I suppose I ought to feel pleased that you seem to think I'm God. When your father died, I was here in Colorado, fighting a war. These are violent times. People go wild. Your father did something stupid. And I'm—you won't believe this—I'm genuinely sorry."

"What about this man Durgas?"

"He had nothing to do with it. What do you know about him?"

"He does your dirty work for you."

"That wasn't dirty work."

"You never knew they'd caught him?"

"All right. I knew that. But—"

"And there was nothing you could do?" Her voice had become shrill; she was shouting, nearly hysterical. He knew he ought to order drinks. But, to do that, he'd have to leave.

Would she allow him back?

So what he tried to do was tell her the true facts surrounding her father's death. Late in August, Daniel Malone and two other men had been apprehended near the Canadian border while trying to flee the country with a suitcase stuffed with gold and various securities. The Nationalists had been chasing them too, but it was a Red guerilla band that had captured them. The men were sneaked into Minneapolis and jailed there. The Nationalists were then still in control of the surrounding countryside, while the city itself—and St. Paul too—was firmly in the hands of the Red forces. The Nationalists had halted all food shipments into the city and the population, growing hungrier and more desperate daily, needed something close at hand to blame for their plight. Rumors started and spread. The three prisoners were Nationalist spies; worse than that, they were food hoarders on a massive scale. Meetings were held; crowds became angry mobs. Two days after the arrival of the prisoners one such mob descended upon the city jail. The men were removed, beaten, finally hanged. The mob then dispersed. Three days later, following uprisings in Chicago and Detroit, the troops blockading Minneapolis were withdrawn. The people once again were able to eat. The three dead men had long since been forgotten.

"Did they try to stop them?" she asked.

"The mob? No."

"Didn't they have guns?"

"Yes, but so did the mob. And they were our people, Rachel. Your father wasn't."

"So you had him killed. You admit it."

"I did not. Don't be ridiculous."

"You told me when I first met you that you wanted to kill him."

"That's not true."

"You hated him."

"So did you."

"Good." She seemed to turn instantly calm, all evidence of impending hysteria gone. "I want you to do something with me," she said.

"Anything," he said.

"Then go away with me. Anywhere, just not here. Even Russia. I can't stand this place any longer. Running, running, always running. Cities. Hotel rooms. I've got to get out of here."

He shook his head. "Rachel, that's impossible. After the fighting is over—only a few more months at the most—I'll take you anywhere for a vacation."

"I mean now."

"No."

"I mean for good. Not a vacation."

"And give up everything? Quit? I can't do that."

"Why not? You told me yourself it's nearly over. Your place in history is safe. You've done your part for the proletariat. Now turn it over to Ennis, or Durgas, any of them. They all want power. Share some of it with them."

"No."

"You want it all for yourself."

"It's not that." He shook his head. "Not power. What I want is—you won't understand—revenge."

"You're right. I don't understand."

"I wish I could explain."

"You won't?"

"I can't."

"Then you'll have to get along without me. I'm leaving you, Tommy."

"I won't let you."

"You'll have me killed?"

"Stopped. I'll have you locked up."

"You love me that much?"

"Maybe I do."

She laughed at him. "You liar. You don't love me, you need me. Admit it."

"All right. Sure. I suppose it's a matter of image. A leader in America is supposed to have a wife. You're mine. So that's the way it's going to have to be."

"I'm glad it's been decided. I'm sorry you were too busy to ask me how I felt. But for right now I won't argue with you. I won't whine or beg or get down on my knees and pretend to pray. Just get out of here. You've done your duty, now go. Get out. Leave me the hell alone." She rolled over, tucking her face close to the wall. He heard her breathing, a quiet sound, calm, like waves on a tranquil sea.

He went to the door, opened it, then turned back.

She was watching him. Their eyes met, and for the first time since waking, he was prepared to share the truth with another person—with her: that he had died once and been reborn, that he now had no choice but to devote the whole of his new life to ensuring that the death which had once struck him down would not occur in this world too. I am not a man whose life is his own to choose and direct. I must accomplish those acts for which I was reborn. If the choice were mine, perhaps I would go with you. But that choice is not mine; the decision was made for me eleven years ago—thirteen years from now. I'm sorry, Rachel. I'm sorry.

But she had turned away again. He saw he had waited too long, that it was over now.

So he went out the door and back to the lobby and asked the captain to call for a car. He added, "And see if you can find something for Mrs. Bloome to drink. I don't know what she likes. Anything strong. Don't ask her, just take it to her room. And do it yourself."

"I understand, sir."

"You do?"

"Well, yes—I mean, no."

"Sure."

Outside, the sky was as clear as before but the moon had dropped from view. Tommy stood on the porch, ignoring the presence of the guard, guessing that he ought to be cold; the wind was blowing hard. But he wasn't cold. He felt just fine. Puckering his lips, he tried to make a ring with his frozen breath. But you couldn't do that. Air wasn't smoke. Air could not be controlled.

The lights of an approaching car breached the darkness. Twin yellow lights bounded through the night. The car arrived. Tommy got in, saying,

"Home."

Chapter Nine

She had gone with him to the front door and now stood poised, one hand on the doorknob, saying, "Good-bye, Bob."

"Good-bye, Rachel."

Her other hand went toward the light switch. But he grabbed her wrist gently and pulled her hand down.

"Don't—they may be out there."

"Oh, I'm sorry. I—"

"Yes, I know. Forget that. But when I go out, what you'd better do is turn off the hallway light. That way there won't be any light behind me."

"I can do that."

"Good."

"But do you really think he expected you to come here? If he did, that makes him smarter than me. I never expected to see you again in my life."

He laughed kindly. "Where else could I go, Rachel?"

"That woman. I can't remember her name, but I do recall you saw her a lot back in San Francisco. You got a bar permit for her too. Where was it?"

"Portland. I'm surprised you remember. Lowrey didn't."

"So you did go there." She smiled. "I don't think he knew—about her—Lowrey. You kept a good secret."

He nodded, then reached forward and caught her hand, a gesture of subdued tenderness.

"I've got to go now."

"Portland?" she asked.

"No. That's too dangerous. I don't want them to find out about Molly."

"Then where? You could go to Canada. Or Russia. They'd give you—what's the word?—asylum."

"So would Hitler. But I don't want to live in Germany or Russia. I'm staying here."

"But where?"

"I'm going to the funeral."

"You're mad."

"Maybe I am. But I want to see him buried."

"It's tomorrow. How—"

"I'll find a way. Don't worry." He laid a hand on her lips, cutting off her protest. "It hardly matters if I die anymore. They'll catch me one way or the other soon enough."

She nodded and he released her lips.

Suddenly she laughed. "Maybe I'll see you there. They've put a plane at my disposal. I'm to be on it by nine tomorrow. I don't want to go. Remember when we flew from Boston to Denver that time. How drunk I was."

"You had good reason."

"You think that? Really?"

"He treated you like hell, Rachel. Not just then but always."

"I always thought you hated me."

"Why?"

"Because I kept you from him. You and he had been planning the revolution since the twenties. Then there it was, it was happening, and where were you? On the wrong side of the lines. Stuck in one miserable hotel after another. With a drunk. An old drunken bag."

"I said you had a good reason."

"I'm glad you think so." She let him touch her face, her lips, throat.

"I'm going now," he said.

But she wasn't ready, not yet. The loneliness could come later. She grabbed his hand. "Wait."

He did not resist. "When I came here tonight," he said, "I was thinking of hurting you. It was what I was hearing on the radio—you were crying, sobbing. I knew it wasn't true."

"I'm used to doing what I'm told." She pointed at the door, indicating the darkness beyond. "He's afraid of you, Bob. I thought you ought to know. We talked about you. He said you were the one person who might pose a threat to his power. After the funeral, he's going to announce that you've fled to Germany. Sought asylum with Hitler. He wants to smear your name, call you a traitor. But I don't think he can do that while you're alive to prove him a liar. He's got to kill you, Bob."

"I'm sure he will. But after the funeral."

She sighed, seeing it was impossible to hold him any longer. "Go," she said finally.

"All right."

"I won't forget the light."

"Good."

"I wish you luck, Bob."

"And you too, Rachel."

"Thank you." She stepped back into the hallway, continuing to face him. She had lived in this house since the day she and Tommy had broken for good—since the tenth of April, 1941—and the house had always treated her well. It had belonged to a movie star originally, way back in the twenties —a comedian, he had designed it himself but never moved in. He went broke, his career collapsing before the house was completed. The man was still alive, back in the movies now, though not a big star. Rachel had heard the story of him and the house a thousand times since moving here. It was one of those Hollywood legends. She seldom ventured outside the four walls, the thirty-six rooms, the six acres of the home. She had a big swimming pool, an excellent library, tennis courts, a stable. And there were always people who, when she called and said, "Are you free today? Would you like to have lunch?" would invariably say, "Yes, of course— I'd be delighted, Mrs. Bloome,"

She reached the back of the hall, grabbed the light switch, turned it down. Immediately there was darkness. She held her breath, listening. Had he gone already, demurely silent? "Bob?" she called, but there was no answer.

Carefully she moved forward, hands held perpendicularly in front of her. Reaching the door, she felt the hard wood. There was nothing here.

Turning, she headed straight toward the distant yellow light of the living room and sat down in front of the fireplace, curling her legs beneath her. The fire, which was the only light, had nearly gone out. The clock said it was already past midnight. Time for bed maybe. She wished Ennis all the luck in the world. Poor Bob, good old Bob.

She kicked off her shoes, turned, lay on her back, the

gentle glow of the fire playfully warming her bare arms and cheeks. Her girdle hurt her waist, but she was too tired to change just yet. He had been here when she'd come back from that party: a dinner in Tommy's memory. The comissioner had hosted the event; Lowrey had phoned and ordered her to attend. She rarely went out socially; her presence at any event was a great honor for the host. The dinner had been an ugly bore. Men who had never known Tommy remarked on what a great man he had been. Lowrey was similarly applauded. She was sick of this—the politicians, their empty chatter, discussions of industrial development, food quotas, rumors of war and secret Russian cosmic weapons. Next time Lowrey called to tell her where to go, she would say no. Now that Tommy was dead, she ought to be able to lead her own life. Wasn't that right?

Lifting her hands, she stroked her hair, curling a few stray strands around an ear. The fire was a vaguely felt presence now.

A noise.

She sat up suddenly. What was that? It came again. *Bang-bang-bang.*

Gunshots!

Oh, no. Getting up, she ran to the front window, drew the curtains back an inch, rested her nose in the opening. *Bang-bang.* She saw the flash.

So Lowrey did have the house under surveillance. The bastard. Who did he think—? But why not? she admitted. With Tommy dead, nothing could stop him from treating her in whatever way he desired. He couldn't very well trust her. If Ennis, who was merely Tommy's friend, was a dangerous man to be shot on sight, then what was she? The widow? Couldn't she, with a mere snap of the fingers and a few vague words, plunge the nation into civil war? But did she want to do that? No, of course not. Lowrey could have the whole country. She wanted none of it. She wanted to be left alone.

There weren't any more shots. She waited five minutes at the window . . . ten. Nothing. O.K., she thought, either he got away or he didn't. Either he's out running free or else he's lying on the damp grass of my lawn, dead or dying. There was no way of knowing which until they decided to tell her.

She went back and sat in front of the glowing coals. She glanced at the phone. Five minutes, she thought. That's how long it ought to take for a report to reach him at the Tower. Then, say, another ten minutes for him to get out of bed, wash the sleep from his eyes and mouth, and call her. He would say that Ennis was dead. Whether true or false, that was what he would say. If it were true, then fine, no harm done; and if it were false, then he would be trying to get her to admit (1) that it was indeed Ennis who had visited her and (2) that they had met in order to formulate a definite plan for overthrowing the established state. She wouldn't admit a thing; she'd make him sweat buckets.

"Poor Bob," she said aloud.

But she didn't really mean that. In fact, she was pretty sure he wasn't dead. It was dark out there. Ennis was fast and smart. She was nearly positive she would be seeing him again tomorrow at the funeral. Lowrey would get him after that, but if Ennis did not care, then neither did she.

The phone remained silent. Funny. Her time limit had passed and then some. Maybe Lowrey had gone to the bathroom and gotten tangled in his pajamas. She laughed at the image of that and felt much better.

Then the phone rang. She stood up and listened to the shrill rhythmical blasts of sound. Three rings. Four. A fifth. Six. On the seventh ring, she moved. Here came number eight. She felt her dress, smoothing the folds across her flattened belly. Nine. She crossed the room. Ten. She lifted the receiver, placed it against her ear.

"He's dead," said Arnold Lowrey.

"So?"

"They shot him, all right. Got brains splattered all over your lawn. So you may as well tell me what he wanted there."

"Who?" she asked coolly.

"Come on, Rachel, honey."

"Are you talking about Tommy? Is that why you woke me up in the dead of night? Tommy Bloome is dead. I know that, Arnold. I was there—I stuck a pin in his heart to make sure."

"You know damn well who I'm talking about, Rachel. There was a tag out on him. I could have you run in as an accessory. You could be shot. Harboring a fugitive."

"Oh, oh, oh," she said, pretending enlightenment. "Carstairs. But, Arnold, a tag? On—"

"You shut up." There was a lengthy pause during which Rachel heard only his fierce, ugly breathing. "What are you talking about?" he said, at last.

"The man your men were shooting at tonight. Carstairs Kennedy. Didn't you bother to find out who he was? Surely you remember Carstairs. An old New York friend of mine." She spoke rapidly, loudly, slipping easily past his attempted interruptions. "Did you really kill him? Carstairs? Christ, Arnold, what's wrong with you? He was the most harmless man alive."

"That's enough, Rachel. I mean that—you can just cut it out. I'm talking about Bob Ennis."

"Oh, you mean Ennis is dead. Well, I never doubted you'd get him. Why tell me?"

"Because he was there. His body is out on your lawn right now."

"You put a body on my lawn?"

"I said that was enough, Rachel."

"But it'll stink. Arnold, I really wish you'd find another place. I—"

"Enough!"

She said softly, "Are you sure?"

"Yes."

"Then I think it might be a swell idea if I stayed home tomorrow."

He was trying patience now. "What would that prove?"

"Oh, maybe nothing. Or maybe that I don't like having my friends shot down."

"O.K. I'll tell you what—I'll level with you. Ennis ain't dead. We shot at him, but it was dark and we missed. How's that?"

"Very candid. But it was Carstairs Kennedy you shot at."

"Kennedy is dead, Rachel."

"What?"

"He died two years ago on his farm. TB."

"Well," she said, allowing him his moment of victory.

"So you're going to have to think up a new name, Rachel, and it better be Bob Ennis. So you can tell me what it was he wanted."

"The man was my gardner. Sam Cortez. A little man but strong. I told you it was Carstairs because I didn't want you to know how low I've fallen."

"You fired Cortez six months ago."

"Ah, but that was a subterfuge. To get you off the scent. He's still here, sleeps right in my bedroom with me. I sent him to the store for cigarettes, but now he'll probably be afraid to come back. Damn you, Arnold."

This time Lowrey said nothing. He had realized she wasn't going to talk to him.

"All right, you win. Just be on that plane tomorrow."

"I wouldn't miss it for the world. Is that all?"

"That's all."

"Then bye-bye."

She dropped the phone. God, that was fun. She went to the couch and threw herself down like a schoolgirl, laughing, kicking her feet.

God, she hated Lowrey. Did she ever. She hated him so much it was funny. Getting up, she tossed another log on the fire, watching the flames flicker, spread, glow.

She turned, thinking, If I could, I would. If only I could. She sat down on the couch.

A way to make him pay. To fix him for good. She thought and thought. A way.

The fire rose, burned, fell, rose again as she added another log. She continued thinking. The fire went up and down. Thinking. And drinking. She found a bottle and poured glass after glass. Gin. She took the situation of this singular moment and turned it in her mind, carefully considering each of its myriad and vital aspects. She became a snowflake. How strange.

She saw. Why hadn't she seen before? It loomed so vast and clear. But bent, slightly askew. Well, she saw it anyway; she knew.

Outside, the sun popped above the horizon. The house burned with light. She went over to the window and drew back the shades and then, as daylight spread languidly across the empty lawn, she reached behind and unzipped her dress. Her shoes were already off. She squirmed out of her girdle, laughing at the ticklish sensation. Her breasts hung down as she peeled her stockings off.

In panties only—narrow at the hips, snug and full behind—Rachel went outside. Hello, hello. A kind and sunny day, rich and promising. She stepped to the center of the lawn, ignoring—in the distance—the black smear of a highway. Off came her last lace garment. Naked, Rachel stood there, feeling half her real age, feet apart, arms raised high, head tilted back. Her hair fell down, way down, past her smooth shoulders.

Then she ran around the house. Grass tickling wetly between her toes. They were out here, weren't they? The men. Weren't they seeing her now?

She came to the pool, stopped, leaned down, peered at the pale reflection that danced upon the blue waters. How strange. Rachel past forty, but as bare as the original babe.

Hello.

She waved at herself.

What's new? Hi, hi, hi.

She stepped back, sighing. Enough was enough. Day was done. Gone.

She was afraid she was going to cry.

She ran. The house opened to swallow her. In the doorway she stopped, turned, stood poised on tiptoes, then finally waved.

No one answered.

She waved again.

Still, nothing.

Then, demurely, unaware of her nakedness, she turned and entered the house.

The door closed.

Rachel was gone.

Chapter Ten

The first woman who could claim to have known Arnold C. Lowrey and known him well was the boy's mother, Anna. Her hands were red sores dangling from the ends of pitchfork skinny arms, flesh as white as a cloud, with a pair of huge brown eyes and white-gray hair that sprouted rather than grew in thin wispy tufts from the peak of a narrow pointed skull. Anna loved her son Arnold with deep and honest devotion, though devoid of any passion or tenderness. The fact that the boy's father had gone away before Arnold turned five, asserting as he went a patriotic need for prompt enlistment in the United States Marine Corps, which was then on its way to the island of Cuba in order to fight a brutal Spanish enemy which, among other atrocities too numerous for detailing, had knowingly stripped innocent young Cuban aristocrats (that is, ladies) down to their bare, corset-tightened waists and then searched them thoroughly with knowing Latin hands—this absence of the father neither increased nor lessened the love of Anna Lowrey for her son. Some of those who knew the elder Lowrey best (including his eight legitimate brothers) later said, not smiling, that Carlton Lowrey had willingly surrendered his liberty to an alien government—that of the United States—merely in hopes of managing, somewhere on the Havana waterfront, to catch a glimpse, however faint or fleeting, of a single brown budding Cuban aristocratic nipple. But no matter what explanation one accepted, whether Carlton Lowrey's own or that of his friends and brothers, the fact remained that, come March of 1902, by which time the war had long ago been won and the ladies of Cuba again decently clad, with the grandest hero of that awful conflict firmly established in the White House, Carlton Lowrey had not returned home. So, with the help of her son, who could write somewhat better than herself, Anna Lowrey penned a letter of inquiry to this hero and President, asking, dear sir, if he might possibly recall a certain Carlton Lowrey, a Marine recruit, might have some idea of what had happened to him, dead or missing or prisoner of war, though realistically she suspected desertion, receiving in reply a brief note from the Department of War which informed her simply that no record existed of any such Lowrey in any such war and that she ought to write directly to the secretary if she had any further information on the man.

Anna never showed this letter to a soul but, having now done her proper duty as a wife, shrugged her shoulders and forgot completely about the missing Lowrey. Life without him proved to be neither better nor worse than before, and Anna continued to labor daily with fierce desperation beneath the uncompromising Arkansan sun in order to get her crops done in time. The farm (as only Anna ever dared call it) was merely a share. The deed rested in the time-locked vault of a banker named Weston, who along with a county full of sons and daughters and nephews and cousins, owned most of the rest of this part of the state as well. The neighbors of Anna Lowrey were a bitter and aimless lot, the faces of whom, male and female, wore a covering skin as thoroughly black as the soil in which they worked. Anna had no time for friends. Before she was sixteen, her own family had died out; Carlton's brothers had their own problems. Except for the boy—for Arnold—she was alone and isolated. She never noticed this fact.

When Arnold was fifteen, Anna Lowrey died, but before doing so she told him something he never could forget afterward. It was a strangely silent night, surely winter, with a fire burning in the small fireplace and a wind ripping through the walls of the cabin. Anna sat in her broken-legged rocking chair. Below, curled at her feet, Arnold was reading a battered book, the family Bible.

Suddenly, she said to him, almost screaming, "Get out!" He looked up, staring coldly. "You get out!" she cried. "As soon as you're old enough and I am dead, you have got to promise me that you will do that one thing: you will leave. I do not want you to stay in this accursed place, where you would rot and die like all the rest of them, of us." Gripping his shoulder tightly, her raw red hand shaking with passion.

"Please, Arnold, you have got to tell me that. You will leave. Promise me. Do it now, now."

"I promise," Arnold said softly, very softly, firmly aware of the significance of this moment. "I will do it."

She kissed him.

Anna never again referred to this subject, but Arnold never forgot his promise. Maybe it was the fact that he had not only got away but gone so far that caused him to remember that entire scene thirty years later with astonishing clarity. *I promise—I will do it.* And he had.

After his appointment as Second Director of the Free Democracy of the United States, Arnold C. Lowrey made a last visit to the old place down in Arkansas. Standing beside the big black limousine, he peered across the flat ruptured land to the rotting cabin, where a Negro family of ten (including both grandmothers) presently lived, trying to earn —hardly any different from Anna Lowrey—a meager living from that harsh soil. He spent the whole morning and afternoon there, standing, simply watching, the Negroes ignoring him as completely as if his white skin had succeeded in rendering him invisible. That evening Arnold drove back to Quincy and, pounding on the banker's door, succeeded in depositing ten thousand anonymous dollars in the bank account—newly opened—of that Negro family back there. Why? For what reason? Nostalgia? Guilt? He didn't know—his mind never entered these realms. But, outside of the place it occupied in his official biographies, Arnold C. Lowrey never visited or mentioned Quincy, Arkansas, again and, so far as he was consciously concerned, it ceased to exist except as a very tiny dot on the map.

Arnold did not leave the land till nearly three years after his mother's death. In staying, he managed to graduate from the local high school—no mean accomplishment for a sharecropper's son in those years—but this was not the reason. On the surface, he stayed in order to work for Thom Weston, whose father owned the Quincy bank, attempting, supposedly, to pay off a large debt left by his mother, but this was not the reason either. By working for Weston, Arnold received a roof over his head (Weston's barn) and three good meals each day, but these were not reasons. The real reason, the one and only true reason why he stayed, was a woman, a girl, the second of his life.

Her name was Missy, breasts big and high and colored like peaks of dark petrified wood, granddaughter of a living ex-slave named Mary Kingsley and of Percy Weston, founder of the Quincy bank.

Arnold was not the first local boy to meet with Missy in some private place, but he was the only one who ever took her to the secret, sheltered place far off the main county road where a deep flowing brook rushed briefly between the state-ly sweeping trunks of a hundred Arkansan pine. And the grass was pure green—so he saw it in memory—never a speck of brown or yellow even at the height of summer, and Missy told him one afternoon that he was the only boy who never asked or expected her to do certain things she would not even consider doing, and she respected him deeply for that, she knew he wasn't any common man. In truth Arnold never asked or expected Missy to do anything, respectable or not, but rather crawled diffidently between her waiting thighs, his rope-belted trousers down around his ankles, her dress hitched high to the neck, exposing to the pine-smelling air the beauties of her finely carved chocolate breasts, and he would move so softly and shyly inside her that sometimes she would think he had fallen asleep and, as they lay to-gether, the sun often passed from high in the sky and crawled behind the trunk of one of the higher trees before, with a groan, Arnold would come, turn, roll away, his back turned toward Missy, and he would peer into the waters of the brook and when asked would reply that he was merely watching the big fish way down deep in the water where no human eye was supposed to be able to see them. He never asked Missy for a thing, seldom spoke except in reply to a direct question. Strictly speaking, he used her, fucked her, but the actual truth was that he loved her as well, and for this reason—and this reason only—he stayed in Quincy.

Until one afternoon:

"I've got to be going."

"You mean now?" she asked.

"I mean for good. I have got to get away from this place."

"Why? Is it something I did? Or you? Did you go and do something to somebody you oughtn't to've tried?"

"No. It's nothing like that. It's just that I want to get away. I feel it's the time, so I better go now."

"And you won't ever come back, will you? Tell me now. I've got a right to know."

"I won't ever come back. Not ever."

This was when Missy began to cry and when Arnold, then eighteen, reached and took her, then seventeen, in the cradle of his arms and held her close to his breast with a tenderness he never knew he possessed, more gently and truly than any husband with his wife, and he told her, truthfully, that the only reason he had stayed these three years was because of her, because he had guessed this would be his one and last time, and that after this he would never be able to find such peace with another. But still he had to go now.

"But why?" she asked.

"Because if I stay here I will die."

"You have got some sort of sickness?" she said, wide-eyed with concern.

"No."

"Then I don't understand you at all, Arnold Lowrey."

By the time Arnold left her, Missy was standing as straight as she could, spine already bent from years of stooping, bending, picking, a seventeen-year-old girl who, in less than ten years, would bear a total of eight children and who would die, in some twelve years time, while bringing forth a ninth and final descendant, but she wasn't crying; there wasn't so much as a trace of spent wasted years in her hard unyielding eyes. She let him go, watched him go, then crept through the tall whispering grass to the edge of the brook and stood there dead still till the sun dropped behind the horizon and then, suddenly afraid, she screamed, turned, ran for home, falling once, slicing her ankle upon a jagged rock. All that time, while Missy stood beside the brook, she had been peering deeply into the depths of that dark water, wanting to see, striving and seeking, somehow knowing that any conceivable solution must lie here. It was as near as Missy was ever to come to touching and seeing the god in whom she endlessly believed but, in the end, she found nothing there—just water.

That night, Thom Weston came to see Missy's father and told him he was being evicted from his share, and that same night Arnold Lowrey left the Weston barn and caught a ride with a farmer to the county seat of Melville, a village of some twenty thousand souls. Before going, Arnold met briefly with his mother's one surviving relative—a distant cousin —a consultation that gained Arnold a written recommendation for a job in Melville working for a cousin of the cousin. Arnold was to sell farm equipment. He took the job gladly enough, seeing a sort of freedom in this simple, casual work, and he did it for some four years, and by the end of this time the innocent, constantly smiling, shy country boy from Quincy was quite dead; in his place stood a bright beaming outgoing bubbling backslapping city salesman who wore white suits and wide ties and a straw hat tilted over one eyebrow and who was already building an armor of fat around his face and neck and belly. At the end, he had a full crew of thirty men and boys working directly under him, selling not only farm equipment but also shoes, socks, jewelry, horse meat, Bibles, over a five-county area. His own duties by then were limited to slapping backs, rubbing elbows, and swapping filthy stories, but he chose to do more than this —much more.

The woman involved was Kathryn Curtis, known as Kate, wife of the lawyer Jefferson Curtis, in whose home Arnold lived during the final two years of his stay in Melville. Lawyer Curtis had met Arnold in some vague fashion neither could later recall and, instantly impressed, had offered the young man a clerical position in his firm and, shortly after that, the use of the extra guest room in his own home. Lowrey, slyly, waited until the second offer was made before refusing the first, preferring the contacts he made on the road to any he might later make in a court of law; without hesitation, working from sharply toned intuition, he accepted the second offer and moved into the empty room that very night. He discovered Kate during his third week, not surprised that she proved to be as violent in bed as she was refined out of it. Jefferson Curtis was a bald-headed, sweating man who had met his bride, twelve years his junior, while attending the law school at Yale University. Kate Curtis, arriving in Melville, was shocked to learn that she would not be permitted to enter the normal flow of the town's society simply because of the happenstance of her birth in the state of Massachusetts. For years she nursed her grudge, keeping her bitterness and loneliness strictly to herself, finally replying to the town's hatred with a benevolence worthy of an apostle by taking one of Arkansas's own, Arnold Lowrey, into her bed.

Kate loved Arnold with real vengeance. While Jefferson obliviously slept a mere two doors down the hallway, Kate would lie abed, stroking Arnold's bare chest, whispering to him that, oh yes, she loved him, he was exactly what she needed to survive and thrive, and he would lie beside her, puffing on a big black cigar, the ugly odor of which never wholly left the room, asking, "Why do you tell me that? What am I to you except some young bull ram of a stud? You go and tell me that."

And Kate would say, "You're going places. I've never met a man quite like you. You're the talk of the town."

"How the hell would you know that, since the town won't ever talk to you?"

"Jefferson says so too."

"I'm nothing but a salesman."

She laughed. "And you're selling yourself, selling Arnold C. Lowrey. Don't try to fool me."

When he was twenty-three, Arnold left Melville and went to the state capital in Little Rock, where he served a session as legislative aide to the newly elected state senator from Melville, Jason Bond, a dapper little man with cufflinks the size of the whites in a nigger's eyes (Bond's own comparison), Jefferson Curtis's law partner, who had known all along exactly what must be occurring beneath the roof of the Curtis home and who, with his electoral victory, had finally found a means by which to extricate Arnold Lowrey from the eye of his chosen storm. Or, as Bond put it to a friend, "Someday Jefferson is going to stumble into that room without knocking, and when he does, no matter how he feels, his pride is going to make him put a hole through that whore's white head."

Arnold made no objection to the change. In truth, he had lately begun to weary of old Kate. The provincialism of Melville was a further constraint; Little Rock proved to be a whole new wider world. Like most pioneers, Arnold immediately set out to conquer this virgin land. Beneath Kate Curtis's soft, soothing hands, he had developed a powerful emotion—no doubt always present—which had grown to dominate and soon obliterate all others; this emotion was called ambition.

With the devoted dedication of a born scholar, Arnold Lowrey studied the world of Little Rock. *Know—then conquer,* that might well have been his motto. After Kate, women were relegated to a minor place in his life. He knew them now. It would no longer be possible to describe his life in terms of the women he had known. A wife would come later, but he hardly bothered to know her either.

During his first legislative session in Little Rock, Arnold studied every handshake. He stood aside while Senator Bond accepted several small bribes and one quite large one. He watched while Bond joined with the majority in quietly defeating a bill providing free textbooks to the state's poor children. On another day he saw the state's corporation taxes, never very large, abolished without protest. At the end of the session, Senator Bond fired him for various unstated reasons and warned him further not to return to Melville. With daring ease Arnold caught on with another senator, one slightly more honest and inestimably wiser than Bond. Arnold learned a lot now. After two sessions with his man, he returned to Melville, ignoring Bond's threats, and stood for election to the state's lower house. In the Democratic primary he defeated the incumbent by a margin of forty-three votes after campaigning in every nook of the district, excepting Quincy, where he still refused to return. He talked rich versus poor and money versus need and how the whole state was owned and run by a crackerbarrel full of carpetbagging crooks from New York and Chicago and Philadelphia. Sometimes he let loose and told his listeners the whole truth—more often lies served equally as well—but he won, and that was the important thing, forty-three votes or not. The people believed what he told them. The techniques he used were those he had developed during his years of selling chicken wire and King James Bibles. When he was offered two thousand dollars to quit the race, he said sure, of course, you bet, and took the money, then publicized the arrangement through a friendly newspaper, neglecting to mention the actual consummation of the deal, and demanded, from the stump, the immediate arrest and prosecution of Senator Jason Bond, who, said Arnold, had instigated the obscene offer.

He found running for office to be a great deal of fun and, unlike what everybody said and expected, he did not settle down once installed in office. He kept right on having fun, making his speeches, haranguing his crowds of honest men. Returning to Melville during a reelection campaign, he took Kate Curtis to bed, and she asked him, "What are you trying to prove down there? Don't you know how they hate you? A day doesn't go by without someone suggesting—and I mean an important man—that you are related to Satan himself and ought to be hanged. There is even a rumor that you had a Negro mistress in Quincy and they ran you out of town over it. Why do you insist on fighting men who can fight back? Jason Bond would kill you himself. You have the rabble on your side but they are fickle men. Read some history, Arnold. You're playing with fire."

"They believe in me," he said smugly. "I stand for what they believe."

"But what does that prove?"

"How do I know? Maybe, maybe it proves this: that a little orphan boy from the country can go far—I mean very, very far—like maybe all the way to being the President of the United States."

Her laugh was hollow. "My, you are ambitious."

"Watch me," he said.

On his second try, in 1928, Arnold Lowrey became governor of Arkansas. By this time he had acquired a wife and two small daughters, political necessities in any truly Christian state, and a fair amount of money too. He moved his family into the governor's mansion, made sure everyone had a room and a maid, then scurried across the street to the legislature and presented a program that deliberately included at least one concept guaranteed to shock and disgust every one of the state's myriad special interests. The reaction in the weeks that followed made him laugh. He knew he had the people on his side. He thought of the promise he had made his mother and told her, speaking silently, "Now see how far your boy has come. And look, he ain't through moving yet."

He passed his program too. When a bill was up for debate, Arnold would stand at the back of the chamber, flashing blatant signals to selected henchmen among the legislators. Highways were passed, textbooks for the poor, free lunches for hungry pupils, and a statewide system of medical assistance to the aged and indigent. But this was only the beginning. In the next session in order to pay the cost of his programs Lowrey recommended a huge increase in state taxes, the largest of which would be a tax upon corporate income.

The result of this proposal was impeachment. Money immediately began to flow through the legislative corridors like water through the nearby Mississippi River. For six weeks charges against the governor were heard by the state senate. But Arnold had his private fortune; he had wealthy friends who had chosen to tie themselves politically to him. So when the buying and selling was finally done and the senate chose to vote, Governor Lowrey held on to his office by a margin of two votes. An election followed and there was Arnold dashing around the state in a touring car, visiting every district represented by an opposition legislator, waving sheets of paper at crowds of men and women barely able to read, telling them bluntly and frankly, proclaiming the raw, undiluted truth. "Here in my hands is evidence of what I've been saying. This fellow who is supposed to be representing your interests in our state capital—each and every one of you regardless of the amount of money you've got in your pocket—it says right here that this fellow put into his own pocket ten thousand dollars of money belonging originally to the Reynolds-Malcolm Manufacturing Company. Now who the hell are they? you might want to know. Do they live and work around here? Well, I'll tell you. It says right here on this sheet of paper: it says New York, New York. And not just there. No, sir. It also says Chicago and Boston, Massachusetts. But here in Arkansas? No, sir. I'm looking and I see nothing about Arkansas. Now I'm asking you folks, who is this fellow really representing up there in Little Rock? How come he voted to take my job away from me even though you people had said you wanted me in there? Is it you or is it—maybe—these folks up in New York City who are so freely giving away ten thousand dollars it takes you ten years or more to earn? But now it's your turn to vote and, before you do, I think you ought to ask yourselves a few of these questions. Ask them, then answer them, then go vote. I got nothing else I can tell you."

By 1932 Arnold C. Lowrey held the state of Arkansas so firmly in the grip of his bare hands that, had he wanted, he could have given it a sudden squeeze and choked every man and woman in the population to death.

Nor was he finished yet. The Great Depression was an event made to order for Arnold Lowrey and he began to speak in different and distant parts of the country. He became a national celebrity and often spoke over network radio. He advocated taking money from the rich and giving it to the poor and found—not to his surprise—that this position was popular with men of all walks of life, excluding a few millionaires and their lawyers.

In Chicago in 1932 at the Democratic convention, Arnold and his handpicked delegation backed the crippled governor of New York, Franklin Delano Roosevelt, who missed winning the necessary two-thirds majority needed for nomination by twenty-six votes and when the deadlocked convention, after brief flirtations with Al Smith and John Nance Garner, settled upon Ohio's compromise candidate Newton D. Baker, Governor Lowrey led his Arkansas delegation stomping out of the hall. Pausing upon the sidewalk, he told a throng of reporters that the United States presently stood upon the brink of violent revolution. "The last chance for honest men to save this country as we have known it for a hundred and fifty years has failed today. The men with the money have decided to stick their heads in the sand and bury the rest of us along with them. Nobody won inside that hall today except maybe the communists. We all lost. I'm going home and I'm sorry."

He went home, ran for the U.S. Senate, won by a simple landside, and saw a former member of his cartel of salesmen elected to the vacated governorship. He didn't like Washington especially much but thought that it might prove bearable when, in 1936, he was elected to the White House.

But Tommy Bloome's revolution, which Arnold had often predicted but never expected, spoiled all of that. Assembling a crew of cronies, Arnold ran fast for the hills and hid out there, drinking whisky and playing poker and screwing whores imported from Little Rock. The revolution went on outside. He ignored it as much as possible, unconcerned over the final victor. If the Nationalists won, he expected they would shoot him, but he didn't think the Reds would treat him any better. So when Bloome finally emerged the winner, there was nothing Arnold could do but shrug his big shoulders and head back for the capital. He occupied an office in the governor's mansion, hired several dozen bodyguards, and waited.

Two weeks after his return, a secretary entered his room and said, "Senator Lowrey, there is a man here who wishes to speak with you."

"Do I know him?"

"No, sir. I don't believe so."

"Then tell him to go about his business."

"He says he represents Tommy Bloome, sir." The secretary spoke this name cautiously, as though it were a fearful object to be approached only on tiptoe.

"Bloome, uh?" Lowrey scratched himself. "Well, that's interesting." Draining his whisky glass, he turned to the mob of cronies who crowded the room and said, "All of you go out and take a walk." Then, as they left, he asked the secretary, "This fellow have a name?"

"He said he was John Durgas."

"O.K. Then let's see him."

Durgas entered the room, nodded at Lowrey, and waited patiently for the secretary to depart. On sight, Lowrey detested and distrusted this tall dark man with the pale slender lips.

"Are you here to arrest me?" Lowrey asked. "Or should I offer you something to drink?"

"No," said Durgas.

"No, what? No drink or no arrest."

"No, both."

"Well, that's a good start," Lowrey said. "But maybe you ought to tell me exactly what you do want here." Lowrey watched with amused satisfaction as Durgas surveyed the room, searching for a seat. There were three chairs but all were situated in various corners of the room where any visitor would be placed at an awkward disadvantage in relation to the man behind the desk. Durgas stepped back and leaned against the wall. He crossed his arms casually over his chest and smiled.

"I want to offer you a job."

"Digging ditches?" said Lowrey.

"In Washington."

"Ditches?"

"You'll be required to swear your loyalty to our new party."

"I already have—two weeks ago." Lowrey tried a smile himself. "Did Bloome really send you here?"

"I came purely of my own accord."

"Then how about, on your own accord, getting out of my office?"

Durgas remained as calm as ever. His smile remained firmly intact. He shook his head. "Don't be an ass, Lowrey. Bloome will want you. I can guarantee there will be no difficulties. We need a man in our government, in a fairly prominent position, with some connection to the past. A man connected, if you sense my meaning, but not tainted. I have considered all the possibilities open to us and you happen to be the man we need. The Republicans and Democrats are equally tainted. We do not like Socialists. I want you."

"I'm not as stupid as I look," Lowrey said. "You may be taking a risk."

"I am aware of that. But you should be aware of this: you will be alone. Every other man in the government will be a Bloome loyalist."

"Does that include you?"

"Of course it does."

"Then what is this job. Specifically?"

"Specifically, it is nothing. We will see that you have a title, minister of this or that. You will be expected to deliver speeches, break bottles over new ships. Beyond that, the job will consist of whatever we choose to make it."

"You seem to use a couple of words interchangably. 'We' and 'I.' I want to know, which is it?"

"For all practical purposes, in this matter, they are identical."

"Then I'll take it," Lowrey said.

"I'll have a plane here by nine tonight."

"No plane. A train. And I'll want to bring a few friends with me. Nobody dangerous. I do not have dangerous friends. But I'll need company. If I have to be alone, I do not want to be lonesome too."

"Anything else? A house? Family? Your wife?"

"My wife can stay here. She doesn't like big cities. If you can find me a good-sized hotel with a good-sized suite, I'll live there. And I like to eat good. Check out the dining room."

"Anything else?"

Lowrey shook his head. "Not that I can think of."

"In that case . . ." Durgas smiled, nodded, turned, and left. The door closed and Lowrey found himself alone. He stood and carefully searched the room, hoping to find some clear or definite sign to attest to the past presence of John Durgas. But there was nothing. The man had come and gone with no more substance than a fleeting wraith.

But, at nine o'clock, the train was waiting.

Chapter Eleven

On September 30, 1939, the Supreme Committee of the Free Democracy of the United States voted to appoint Arnold C. Lowrey as Second Director of the Committee, replacing Arthur T. Spine, who had been removed from this same position some few moments before. Lowrey, hearing the announcement of the vote, smiled, accepted the handshakes of his colleagues, and decided the polite and gracious thing would be to wait a day before approaching Tommy Bloome with a certain request.

Lowrey's new offices as Second Director were located on the uppermost, fourteenth floor of the Tower, a gigantic rectangular glass-and-steel building designed by Tommy Bloome himself as a true symbol of the new revolutionary regime —strength, unity, solidarity—and located on the grounds of the old Capitol building. Tommy Bloome's official suite was just down the corridor from the Second Director's office, so when the following day came, it was just a short minute's walk for Lowrey.

"Well, Arnold," said Tommy, who sat behind a modest mahogany desk, hands clasped. A nameplate on the desktop read TOMMY BLOOME, FIRST DIRECTOR. "What can I do for you? Tell me how things are working out."

"Fine, sir, fine," Lowrey said, keeping his feet. "But there is one thing."

"And what is that?"

"My new offices up here. While I do like being so close to you, and consider it both an honor and a privilege, the truth is I sort of like my old office downstairs. Maybe you understand. I've kind of grown attached to the place. It's been—what?—five years now. If I need more room, why not knock down a couple walls, expand things here and there? But I sure do like it down there."

"You like the view," Tommy said.

"Yes, sir. That's right. It keeps me on my toes."

"I imagine it must." Tommy smiled and nodded crisply. "In that case, if it's what you want, go ahead and move back down. I doubt I could get anybody else to move in there anyway. You've jinxed it with your talk. Nobody could sit in there without thinking about the view. You must be the only man I have who likes it on his tiptoes."

"I'm not scared of reality," Lowrey confirmed.

He spent the following week nagging at the workmen who had been sent to enlarge his old office. He told them not to try touching the furniture. He liked the whisky stains, the cigar burns, the places on his desk that had been whittled at with a knife. Finally the men were done and Lowrey could once more sit behind his own desk in his own room. And there was his own window. That was why he had wanted the workmen to finish; it was time to make use of that window again. He glanced at his watch. Just in time. It was only minutes short of two o'clock.

He rang for his secretary, a girl he had inherited from his predecessor, Arthur Spine.

"Yes, sir," came a shrill but not wholly unpleasant voice.

"I want you to come in here," he said.

"Now?" she asked.

"Right now," said Lowrey.

The girl was very dark, her black hair worn shoulder-length. She was around thirty and far from pretty; her front teeth jutted and her nose was long and bent. As she entered, Lowrey looked down and pretended to be reading a handful of papers. He waved at her to sit down beside him, then resumed his reading. It was a British newspaper article concerning his appointment as Second Director. In the text he was described as a "former fascist."

At last he looked at the girl.

She pretended to be eager. "Sir?"

Lowrey spoke sharply, scowling. "What'd you say your name was?"

"It's Rosa Wall," she said evenly.

"You happen to be a Jew?"

"No," she said, glaring at him, eyes filled with hate and disgust. "Are you?"

Smiling, he shook his head. "If you ain't a Jew, then what are you?"

"I'm an American and a Marxist."

"And that means you ain't a Jew?"

"That is correct."

He laughed very loudly, with too much derision. "What's your maiden name?"

"My maiden name is my name."

"Say it again."

"Rosa Wall."

"And you worked for Spine. How long?"

"Three years."

"You knew he was a traitor?"

Her expression now contained fear along with the other emotions. "No," she said softly.

"You were his confidential secretary?"

"Yes."

"Does that mean he used to screw you?"

"If you want to know that, ask the FBI. I'm sure you already have."

"Could be," he said. Standing, he moved around the desk, then suddenly reached out, grasping her wrist firmly. "Come here," he said.

He led her to the window. It was a big window, the glass spotlessly clean, uncluttered by decorative panes. She tried to squirm away but he held her tightly.

"I guess you heard about my window," he said.

"No. Why should I?"

Outside the window, the courtyard at the rear of the Tower could clearly be seen. And, beyond that, the rear wall of the adjacent FBI headquarters. The courtyard was paved, but only two cars were parked out there, each in opposite corners.

"Spine knew. Didn't he tell you?"

"We didn't discuss everything."

"Then take a look down there." He pointed with his free hand and moved close, his cheek brushing hers fleetingly. She drew away in disgust, but he held her wrist firmly and squeezed. Placing his lips against her ear, he whispered, "I'm going to show you something, little girl, so what you're going to do is just watch. Hold still. Stand right up on your tippytoes and look out this here window. That's it. Now you're doing it. Just watch. Look down there."

"I don't see anything," she said from between clenched teeth.

"Don't squirm now. You've got to learn to be patient. That's it. Just look right over there."

He meant the brick wall, an eccentrically placed structure that rose suddenly from the pavement and ran for some ten yards before disappearing as abruptly as it had emerged. The wall was no more than six and a half feet high. The red bricks had been dulled by both sun and rain. From Lowrey's window, standing just right, an observer could see both sides of the wall equally well.

"What time is it?" Lowrey asked.

"Two," the girl said, whispering. "Almost two o'clock. Is that—"

"Hush," said Lowrey. "Watch."

Lowrey stood still, feeling the girl's small breasts heaving against him. He kept trying to remember her first name. Irene? Emily? Rachel?

From a door at the back of the FBI building, a trio of figures emerged and headed across the courtyard toward the wall. Two were big men with broad shoulders, dressed similarly in dark civilian suits. The third man, who stood between the other two, dragged behind. After a few moments of this, the other two grabbed him by the shoulders and pulled him across the yard. This third man wore blue denim overalls. His head was bare, almost bald, but specks of bright red could be seen sprinkled here and there across his skull. Lowrey knew him at once. So did the girl. She stiffened, moaned, tried to break free.

"Shut up," Lowrey said. "You stay here and watch or you'll be down there tomorrow."

"Why?" she cried. "What are you trying to prove? What sort of monster are you?"

The third man was Arthur Spine. For more than four years he had served on the Supreme Committee. For the past two years he had been Second Director. About a month ago, near the tail end of a long and dull committee meeting, Spine had mentioned off hand that it was possible the Free Democracy might soon have to go to war with Japan. Dozens of other men, both in private and public, had mentioned this concept before. Tommy Bloome waited for Spine to finish, then jumped to his feet. His finger pointed as it had so often before. "Treason!" he cried. A moment later the others were shouting the same. Lowrey too. That one word rocked the chamber. "Treason! Treason!" Spine had been suspended from office while his case was reviewed. A jury found him guilty of treason. He was removed from office.

Now he moved slowly across the courtyard, dragged word-lessly toward the brick wall. Lowrey watched the scene without any particular emotion. Years before, the first time he had witnessed this, it had made him sick. Death, he had felt, ought to be a private matter. But he had seen too much by now; too many men had died against that wall. He had stood at this window a hundred times or more and seen men die. He could joke about it. The view kept him on his toes. It was amusing.

Spine stood against the wall. The two big men scurried about, tying leather straps to hold the man—the victim—in place. There was one strap for each wrist, one for the ankles, and another that went around the neck. A blindfold was placed over his head.

The two men stepped back and waited. One lit a cigarette. From the FBI building more men appeared—five, then ten. Each carried a camera. Flashbulbs flared brilliantly. The pic-ture-taking session lasted a minute. The photographers went away, only one allowed to remain. The two big men drew their weapons from their belts. The last photographer raised his camera. The men were five yards from Spine, no farther. They fired together. Six shots, Lowrey counted. The girl screamed with each one. Spine fell, hanging uselessly from the wall. The camera exploded a final time. The blue denim of Spine's shirt was painted bright red. The gunman put out his cigarette and came forward.

"All right," Lowrey said. He released the girl. "Now you saw."

"You bastard," she said. She dropped to the floor and started to cry. Lowrey grabbed her arm and steered her to a corner of the room. He made her lie down upon the couch that was located there. She kicked off her shoes, reached down to cover her exposed calves, then turned her face to the wall.

Lowrey went back to his desk, sat down, and picked up a handful of papers. He read silently.

Shortly the girl stopped crying. She sat up and began to wipe her face.

From his desk Lowrey said, "No doubt you think I'm a mean, vulgar son of a bitch for making you watch that and maybe I am. But I had a good reason. I've had this office with that window for more than five years now. I've seen every damn one of them get shot. I wanted you to see it too because I wanted you to get to feel like me. I wanted to teach you to hate and also how to be scared. If you're going to work for me, you got to know how to do those two things."

She said nothing, simply glared.

"Before you," he said, "I had a secretary who was a real smart girl. She was also a spy. I know you aren't a spy—at least so far. You were Spine's girl, loyal to him, not to them. That's why I asked on purpose that you be allowed to stay here. Otherwise, they were going to send you out west. I said you'd help me in making the transition, but what I want is for you to stay. It was them who killed Spine. That's the part I want you to keep in mind. Hate me as much as you want, but hate them even more."

"I hope you're next," she said. "I want the chance to see you squirming down there. Kill me for saying that if you want."

He shrugged. "I told you what I wanted. Now go think about it. You won't have to tell me what you decide. I'll be able to see from the way you act. Now"—he had suddenly remembered her name—"get out of here and let me work. Rosa."

She left without a backward glance or parting word.

Alone, Lowrey relaxed, sitting deeply in his chair, spine bent in a curve. He was tired. It seemed like, nowadays, he was tired all the time. These past few years had not been easy ones, and sometimes, like now, he couldn't help wondering if all his past actions had really been worth the bother. He could say he was alive. But what else? Anything else? Simply being alive was more than many thousands of his contemporaries could claim, but was it enough? He remembered the first meeting of the Supreme Committee—December 23, 1935—filled with much posturing and proclaiming over the significance of democracy. Fourteen certified revolutionaries had attended that meeting—and himself. How many were alive today? He could count four: Bob Ennis, Rachel Bloome, himself, and Tommy. Ennis was gone from everything except life, purged in 1936, living somewhere out west, they said. Rachel had resigned from the committee in the following year and nobody had seen her since, though it was rumored she continued to share Tommy's quarters in the Tower. Nobody was allowed to penetrate those rooms any deeper than the outer office except Durgas, and Durgas would never talk. Some said Rachel was mad, but who really cared about that? She was gone, that was the significant point, and so it was really only himself and Tommy. Spine had been another, but he was gone now too. And I've got his job, Lowrey thought, his amusement tinged with fear. He didn't want it. As Minister of Culture and then Minister of Finance, he had been able to play his chosen role of hick, fool, buffoon. He had survived, but now that in itself was enough to arouse their suspicions. And when he thought "they" what he really meant was "Tommy Bloome" and that thought gave him another opportunity to laugh and shiver.

It was the pressure and pain of waiting, the constant anticipation, that he hated the most. It was all the things he had to do simply to survive, like with the girl just now. Was death really all that damned awful? He thought that was what happened to some of them. Like Spine. They got tired of waiting and finally said, "All right, death, I've had enough; come and get me."

But Lowrey never got up the nerve to say that, and so he continued to survive. Days passed, then months, and he served his country and leader faithfully. He toured the thriving communal farms of the South and West, he visited the new army posts along the Canadian border, he cracked a bottle of champagne across the bow of a brand new battleship, the USS *Frank Little*. He got drunk (it was expected); he chased women (that, too); he attended his wife's funeral in Little Rock. During the weekly Supreme Committee meetings, he kept his mouth shut, heard briefings, saw films, learned about the war now raging across Europe, the Japanese advances on the Asian mainland. There was Mussolini to consider and Stalin too. Trotsky had been killed at last, Tommy refusing to grant asylum until the end, and Hitler was not only alive but thriving. On the home front a multitude of quotas, both farm and factory, were erected and penetrated. The sixty-hour work week was reestablished; a modern army was conscripted. The nation played at preparing for war, but nobody thought it either imminent or likely; Europe and Asia were too far away. Food graced even the poorest of tables. The horrible winters of '36 and '37, the near-famine conditions prevalent then because of the initial failure of farm communism—those days were already forgotten in the bliss of abundance.

Often now Lowrey met privately with Tommy Bloome, a privilege that frankly worried him. When Tommy spoke, his demeanor was that of a man trying to win over a hostile crowd. In turn, Lowrey often allowed himself to be lulled by the occasion; he spoke too candidly, stating his own opinions rather than repeating Tommy's own.

But he stayed alive nonetheless and, in August, 1940, finally found out why.

He was sitting with Tommy in the latter's office. After an hour's pleasant discussion of a recent uprising of Negro factory workers in the South, Tommy suddenly said, "I think we're going to have to go to war."

Lowrey said, "No!" before he had a chance to think. Recovering partially, he added, "Who with?"

"Germany, of course."

"And Russia too?"

"No. That pact—I know this for a fact—is only a delaying tactic. It won't stand up another year. Durgas just returned from Moscow. They expect to be invaded any time now. Stalin thinks Hitler will wait until after he's beaten the British, but he may be wrong. I don't think we can afford to wait and find out. We have to go over there now."

"Because the Germans will win if we don't?"

Tommy shook his head. "I'm not sure of that."

"Then I don't think I wholly understand you," Lowrey said. "Why is the situation so urgent?"

"They may not win. But they won't lose either. If we get into it, send an army into Europe ten times the size of any we've had in the past, then I think we can beat them. And, if we do, we will dominate the world afterward."

"But why not let them fight each other into the ground? That's not necessarily my point of view, but it's a common one. Germany, Russia, England, France—to a lot of people, they're all foreigners and no concern of ours."

"I'm going to want your help, Arnold."

Lowrey nodded carefully, considering the matter. He asked cautiously, "In what way, Tommy?"

"I'll need help in the committee. Real help. I don't want you to say yes because you're afraid to say no. If you can't follow me all the way, tell me now. You won't be harmed or demoted. I'll respect your private judgment."

"I never said I disagreed," Lowrey said. "I can't claim to be an expert on any of this. Europe is a million miles away to me. I was twenty years old before I got as far as Louisiana."

"That's why I want your help."

"I still don't understand." He tapped his forehead and grinned. "Maybe I'm dense."

"I'll level with you, Arnold. This move is going to be the most dangerous thing I've ever attempted. I've known for years it was going to have to happen, and I've been putting off thinking about it, putting it off. But I can't wait another year, not even another month. I've got to act now. And you're probably the only man in this country strong enough to stop me."

Lowrey shook his head. "You're not supposed to know that."

"But I do. You're a popular man, Arnold. I wouldn't dare try to eliminate you now even if I wanted to. You're a man of the people standing at the top of a strange system few people understand. You're a link to other, easier times. And, right now, I need you more than you ever needed me."

"What about John Durgas? Where does he stand?"

"He's with me."

"Then all right," Lowrey said. After all, there was no other possible course of action. "I'll help you, Tommy."

"You mean that?" There was more than a hint of surprise in his voice.

"Sure, I do."

"Good. Good. Here—hold on a minute." Tommy disappeared into the back and when he returned was carrying a battered cowhide valise. Clicking the lock, he removed a handful of papers and showed them to Lowrey. "In here is a synopsis of everything we presently know about the European situation. I want you to study these documents, memorize them if you have to. When the time comes, I want you to present our argument to the committee. Durgas and I have worked out a strategy to catch them off guard. We'll get them arguing with you, thinking they're agreeing with me, then I'll stand up, throw my support to you, and push through a declaration of war while they're still reeling from shock."

Lowrey smiled appreciatively and said, "I like that." This was familiar terrain—politics. "And it'll damn well work too."

For the next two days Lowrey continued to think this was so, and he kept to his offices, performing only the most routine and tedious chores. On the second night, at nine o'clock, he ordered Rosa Wall to call a car. "I'm going to the whorehouse," he told her. "If anything comes up, you know the number."

"Yes, sir," she said, no less cold than ever.

Earlier in the day he had confided in her. "It's war I cannot accept. Any war. Back in 1898, before you were even born or thought of, my daddy went off to fight in a war and I never saw him again. When I got to be a famous man, governor of my state, I kept expecting to wake up each morning and find that he had come calling. It wasn't so. I knew he was still alive. I could somehow sense his presence out there in the world and knew that he was thinking of me too. So when I got here to Washington I gave his name to John Durgas and asked to have the FBI look for him. Well, finally they found him—out in Colorado—he had been dead two weeks. And when he died, in his pocket there was an envelope stuffed full of newspaper clippings. I've got that envelope in my desk right now. There's newspapers from all over the world—Europe and Asia. And Little Rock too. The clippings were all about me. But he never came to see me. He knew about me but he never even called. Do you know why? If you do, tell me, because I don't know. And it's the same with war. I don't know about that either. And when I don't know about something, don't understand it, then I'm scared of it. And I'm scared of war."

The girls in the small house at the edge of Washington were Southern girls, hardly any past twenty years of age, most brought up from Georgia or Mississippi or Arkansas as part of the Excess Labor Act of 1938 to work in the capital as clerks and secretaries, but these girls, lacking education, had failed their examinations and fallen back into the pool of excess labor. The house had saved them from that dishonor. Now they worked on their backs (usually) at fifty dollars a week (plus tips) and paid an honest income tax to Washington.

He didn't like these girls. Many of them talked back to him. One, a few weeks ago, had called him fat to his face. He used them only because he was a man in the prime of life and knew enough in official Washington to avoid more intimate relations with any normal woman. So he lay atop this tiny wisp of a girl, felt her lips cold upon his neck, dug his fingers—the nails nearly hidden by swollen flesh—into her back, shoulders, ass, and he came on.

Done, he told her, "Get the hell away from me."

She jumped out of bed, threw on a smock, and turned on him, teeth flashing, hand outstretched. "Pay me first."

He searched his trousers, found fifty dollars, gave it to her. "Now get the hell away from me."

"You bet."

Alone, he felt stupid, weak, cold, miserable. Why come here? The act no longer obliterated the pain, barely eased it, did nothing for him. He sighed, stood up, began to dress, his fingers hardly obeying the vague commands of his mind.

Then a knock, a single loud insistent rap.

"Oh, go away," Lowrey murmured. "Away, away, away."

But the door opened. A man passed directly inside, switching on the harsh overhead light as he passed. The door stayed open behind him. A second figure entered: a woman, not young. She stood in the doorway, her eyes swollen holes, her hair a wispy mess. She wore an old, tattered dress at least two sizes too large for her hips and chest.

The man found the chair beside the bed and gestured at the woman to come and sit. She obeyed.

Lowrey thought he recognized her. "You're not Rachel Bloome," he said.

John Durgas answered, "She is."

"Oh, shit," said Lowrey.

"I've been away," Rachel said.

"Tommy had her locked up," Durgas said.

"And you brought her here?" Lowrey had not had time to dictate his own emotions. Anger and fear were already present, but curiosity too, and confusion. "What are you trying to do to me?" he asked Durgas, who stood behind the seated woman, his hands resting casually upon her shoulders. "What is it you want from me?"

"Me, nothing," Durgas said. "But Rachel has something she wishes to ask of you."

Lowrey said, "What?" trying to meet the woman's gaze. But her eyes were not clearly focused; each iris seemed to float aimlessly.

"I want you to make Tommy go away," she said. "We will go back home to San Francisco. I want you to have Tommy's job. Will you take it, please?"

Lowrey shied away from the flatness of her voice. "Get her the hell out of here," he said.

"Now wait," Durgas said. "Listen to her."

"I'm not interested. No, sir." He gained his feet. "You're trying to trap me into something and I'm not—"

"Shut up," Durgas said. "She's here, isn't she? This is Tommy's wife, isn't it? Do you think I'd try something with her? Do you think Tommy would go along with that? Don't be an ass, Lowrey. Shut up and listen."

"No. Uh-uh. The hell with you, Durgas. I'd trust a snake before I'd trust you. I want out of here." He headed for the door.

It was locked.

He whirled, holding the knob vainly. "Open this damn door."

"Listen first." Durgas smiled. "I have two men posted in the hall. Loyal men. No one can get in here or"—smiling more deeply—"get out."

"In ten seconds I'm going to start yelling."

"Why bother people unnecessarily? This is a place of pleasure. Let's not interfere. I can assure you this room is the safest place in the country right now."

"With her in it?" Lowrey came away from the door.

"I had her released from the hospital on my responsibility. You have nothing to worry about."

"The hospital? Is she mad?"

"No more than any of the rest of us. Don't let her fool you. She knows what she's saying, and what we're saying too. Come here."

Lowrey went cautiously forward, tensed to run. Durgas, reaching into his tightly buttoned jacket, drew out a sheaf of papers, which he passed to Lowrey. "Glance through these," he said.

Lowrey loosened the ribbon that bound the papers and read. There were nine statements—each signed by a Supreme Committee member—nine promises. The man vowed that, under certain special circumstances, they would vote to oust Tommy Bloome from leadership. Lowrey was shocked.

"I don't believe it," he said.

"The signatures are quite genuine," Durgas said. He took the statements and returned them to his pocket. "Any hoax should be a simple enough matter for you to expose."

"How did you get them?"

"How? Not easily. But I know my men. I know how to convince them to take certain steps they may want to take but are perhaps afraid to take without a gentle nudge."

"And me?"

Durgas laughed humorlessly. "I don't have a thing on you, Arnold. You're the cleanest man in Washington."

"Then you can't force me, nudge me."

"Did you read the full statement?"

"Yes," Lowrey said.

"Then I don't have to force you to do anything. I'm sure your ambitions will take care of that for me. Upon the removal of Tommy Bloome, you will assume all but the ceremonial functions of his office. Now, tell me, do you mean to say you aren't interested in ruling this country? We all know better than that. Since the day you first came out of the woods, nothing has interested you except the ways and means of acquiring and using power. Well, here's your chance to have more power than any other man in this whole country. Don't tell me you're going to turn it down. Tommy will resign as head of government. You will take his place. It's that simple—and you will have the power."

"He'll never agree," Lowrey said. "He'll fight you all the way."

"No, he won't. With yours, we have ten votes. We have Rachel—and the war. We need nothing else."

"You told them about the war?"

"Why not? It helped convince them of the wisdom of their course. Blackmail, by itself, is rarely enough. Like all dishonest men, our nine friends prefer to think they are acting from honest motives. By ousting Tommy they are preventing the entrance of their country into a huge and ugly war. They are saving thousands of lives. We have here nine men of truly humanitarian principles. I told them you shared their concern for the war and would never send a single American boy to die in Europe or Asia. That's the truth, isn't it?"

"Yes," Lowrey said.

"Splendid." Durgas clapped his hands. "Then everything is so simple. The committee meets tomorrow. I see no reason to delay. I have already drafted the appropriate resolution. When you take the floor to present your war initiative, I suggest you recite a brief listing of the various crimes in office perpetrated by Tommy Bloome. I will see that you have such a list. Move his ouster; I will have arranged a second. I suspect you may well gather a unanimous vote once the others understand the situation. Tommy will be out, you will be in."

"Don't underestimate him," Lowrey warned.

"I'm not. But I know that he will not fight. If he tries, he will lose, and in the course of the fight his loss will be made greater; he will lose his revolution as well as his position, and it is that that he truly cares about. Unlike the rest of us, Tommy Bloome is indeed a man of principles. And, believe it or not, he will trust you to carry on his work. He will step aside. Not without some hesitation, of course. But he will do it."

Lowrey said, "Give me a chance to think." He sank down upon the bed, holding his chin in his hands. After a long moment he raised his eyes and looked straight at Rachel. "How do you feel?" he asked her.

"I feel nothing." Her gaze wavered and suddenly met his. "I want Tommy back," she said. "I don't care about anything else. Say whatever it is you have to say, do whatever you want to do. I need Tommy."

"She's going to give testimony in our behalf. If it's necessary. If he tries to fight. She can say anything and the public will believe it. Tommy made a national heroine out of her during the revolution—fighting the Nationalists from Boston to Oakland, a ring of cartridges around her waist. She's our trump card."

"I know, I know," Lowrey said. He was referring to nothing in particular. "You've thought of everything. So there's just one thing I want to know. You and me. Do you intend to turn me into your puppet?"

"No," Durgas said.

"Then what is the idea? Why are you doing this?"

Durgas shook his head. "Why not?"

"I didn't think you'd tell me. Then get out of here. I think we've said everything there is to say. Take her with you and go."

"Certainly." Durgas raised Rachel by an arm and turned her so that she faced the door. He nudged her gently and she moved obediently forward. Durgas followed. At the door he called his guards. The door was unlocked. Before following Rachel into the corridor, he turned and regarded Lowrey. "Tomorrow," he said softly.

"Tomorrow," Lowrey replied.

Smiling, Durgas waved and went on out.

One day late in 1943 Arnold C. Lowrey sat in his office, skimming quickly through the pages of a thick top-secret report. When he finished the document, he tossed it casually into the open bottom drawer of his desk and considered calling Whistler now. But it was already late, getting close to the time, and he decided to wait until it was over and he was free. Whistler was an assistant in the Ministry of Culture, but what he actually was was the nation's chief fiction writer. Whistler's specialty was Tommy Bloome. In the articles Whistler wrote for the national dailies, he had depicted Tommy in China fighting alongside Mao Tse-tung against the invading Japanese hordes and in London during the worst of the blitz. Presently, according to Whistler, Tommy was serving with the Soviet army in Stalingrad and now it would be necessary for Whistler to compose a piece explaining how Tommy was personally responsible for the recent German retreat from that city. Lowrey considered the possibilities. Tommy could lead a charge against the German lines, an attack so swift and sure that it succeeded in reversing the entire course of the war. Or maybe Tommy could simply convince the mass of the German troops to turn around and go home through the force of his oratory. The report he had just finished perusing contained a considerable amount of background information on the battle. He would have to see that Whistler got a copy. He was proud of his work. He always did careful research. But it was his imagination, his ability to tilt a lie in such a fashion that it never violated the known truth, that made him such a success.

Lowrey glanced down at his watch. There was still time for a quick call. He reached for the phone and dialed three numbers. This was enough to carry his voice across the courtyard into the adjoining FBI building. He told the female voice that answered, "This is the Second Director. I'd like to speak to Mr. Rice, please."

While waiting for the girl to find her boss, he flipped through several more reports. Here was an interesting one. The Chinese communists had won a major battle in the north. A pity Tommy couldn't be there too. And here was another confirming the success of Montgomery's counterattack in Egypt. All the news these days—at least the war news—was turning out unexpectedly well. A pleasant change from the preceding few years. In fact, it was definitely beginning to appear as if the various wars of the world were going to work out for the best, with everyone—Germany, Russia, Britain, Japan, China—losing, and the world's one big neutral—the Free Democracy of the United States—proving to be the ultimate victor.

Lowrey had staked his entire public career—his life, for that matter—on the gamble that this would be so. In 1941, following the Japanese attack on Pearl Harbor and his refusal to declare immediate war, he had dangled at the edge of disaster for months, even after successfully negotiating a non-aggression pact with Japan, before finally managing to consol-idate his strength and win a vote of confidence from the Supreme Committee.

"Hello, Arnold," said the gently accented voice of John Rice. Lowrey had plucked Rice off the University of Ar-kansas campus two years ago and shocked America by turn-ing him into the new director of the FBI. That had been another gamble, but Rice had proved to be a man who knew how to take orders. He was not a fool, nor was he bribable. In the end, Lowrey felt, he had done a damn good job.

"Any problems?" Lowrey asked.

"Not a one," said Rice.

"Delays?"

"You have three minutes. Exactly."

"Good."

"Then you're certain," said Rice, "that you don't want to change your mind? I can still have her removed to—"

"I thought we were both agreed."

"I guess so," said Rice.

"Then let's get it done and over. I'm not going to explain to you. I have my reasons. Believe me."

"Of course I do, Arnold."

"Well, then what about Durgas? Any problems there?"

"I was just going to call you on that. I'm afraid . . ." He hesitated.

"Durgas got loose."

"I'm afraid so. But the men responsible will be—"

"Nope," said Lowrey. "None of that. You let them alone. I'm sure it was none of their fault. You never met Durgas, but I can swear he was the slipperiest man who ever lived. I don't think Superman could have held on to him. In fact, I've got an idea: why don't you call those men—and do it your-self, personally—and tell them I said they done a great job?"

"I'll do that. And while I'm at it, I'll also give them in-structions to shoot him on sight the next time they catch up with him."

"Nope," said Lowrey. "None of that either." Durgas had been captured in Peru, following a chase of more than two years. The pursuing agents had first traced him to Mexico, then into South America—Argentina and Brazil—and then, just as they were about to grab him in Rio, he fled to Europe —occupied France, Switzerland, briefly into Russia. From there, he had managed to sneak back into South America and finally into Peru. No one, least of all Lowrey, knew if there was any point or purpose to this mad chase. "I've decided to forget him. Tell your men they can come home now."

"But—but why? We can still—"

"Still catch him?" Lowrey laughed. "I'm not so sure. But the point is: is he worth the trouble? He can't hurt us. I'm tired of chasing after cheap revenge. Hell, it was Durgas who got me this job in the first place. No, I say let him go. I'm sick and tired of hearing his name."

"Then I'll see that it's done. Anything else?"

"Yeah. The time."

"It's time," Rice said.

"Then I'll talk with you later, John." Dropping the phone, Lowrey stood and went to the window. He looked out, seeing the flat pavement below, a few traces of last week's snow, and by standing a certain way, the red brick wall. The courtyard was normally used as a parking lot nowadays, but it was empty today. Lowrey had ordered that. This ceremony was to be a strictly private event.

He glanced impatiently at his watch. They were late, very late; the phone conversation with Rice had run five minutes over. When he looked up again, he saw that they were coming now. Two men, big men, and between them a woman. Her name, he knew, was Rosa Wall.

The three approached the brick wall quickly. Lowrey was pleased that Rosa did not hesitate. Nor did she display any outward signs of fear or distress. A brave young woman. He was proud of her. She could have been marching to her wedding rather than to her death. Even the ugly prison garments she was forced to wear did not dilute her dignified attitude. Suddenly her head went back and she was looking straight at him. He refused to look away. Of course she knew he was here; he couldn't help remembering that other day years ago when Arthur Spine had died against the wall. But this would be the last time, he reminded himself. After today, that brick wall was coming down. There would never be another. He strained to see her expression, but the distance was too great. What could she be thinking, feeling? He wished there was a way he could know.

One of the men pulled her forward. She fell against the wall. Quickly the leather straps were attached to her arms, legs, and throat. Lowrey glanced toward the phone. There was still time. Should he? Could he? But what if she was doing all this deliberately? If it was an act? She knew him better than anyone since Kate Curtis; she knew how to make him react. He had to think. No, he would not do it. The evidence against Rosa had been too solid. No mistake had been made. Rice had said he was certain and Rice never erred. And Lowrey knew she had always loathed him, had never forgiven or forgotten that first afternoon. For a time, it was true, she had been loyal, but only because she had hated Durgas and Tommy even more than she hated him. But Durgas and Tommy were gone now, and he was left.

Down in the courtyard one of the men was struggling with Rosa, trying to force a black hood over her head. She didn't want it, but the man won, forcing her to accept blindness. He tightened the drawstring at her throat, then stepped back.

No photographers appeared; that part was not necessary anymore.

The two men stood together. They removed their weapons, held them high.

Lowrey whispered, "Fire."

They fired.

Lowrey waited only long enough to see the shots strike home; he saw blood. Then he turned away and went slowly back to his desk. He sat down and waited.

Then, suddenly, his hands flew to his head. The nails dug deeply into the flesh of his brow. He cried out and tried to escape. But his hands kept clawing; they refused to let him go. He began to scream. He cried. But there was no release.

Chapter Twelve

The box that contained the earthly remains of Tommy Bloome was first raised into the air, then lowered down into the waiting earth, slowly, gently, past the green edge of the grass. There was a thud as the heavy wooden coffin came to rest upon the soft bed of the grave.

Hearing the sound, Arnold Lowrey nodded sharply to himself. So it was done now. It was over at last. He stood motionlessly beside the weeping woman, sorely tempted to lean over and tell her she could shut up now. Or, by moving his right foot (the one closest to the woman), raising the heel just slightly, then smashing it down hard and firm and without mercy—that way he could provide her with a dose of real pain, give her something more substantial over which to shed her great puddles of tears.

He felt a smile beginning to form upon his lips, caused by the vision of the howling woman, and hastily reached up to wipe it away. Damn. The television cameras were everywhere. That peeping, prying, constantly spying glass eyeball. It was his own fault for ever authorizing the national network; he should have banned the entire device without a second thought. Fortunately few people were equipped with receivers yet. Still, his advisors insisted, not many years from now there would be millions of sets in the country. He shivered at the thought. That glass-and-metal vulture. Everywhere.

Reaching over, he clasped the woman's hand and pressed hard. He felt her flinch underneath her veil. She wept more powerfully than ever. He released her hand. The camera darted close, as if drawn by an intuition of trouble. He frowned deeply, wiped at his eyes, trying to assume an attitude of mournful grief. He was afraid it was beyond his talents.

The girl beside him—he had to admit this—she was truly splendid. When called upon to speak, her voice had sounded so real even Lowrey himself could not have sworn it wasn't dear dumb dead Rachel he was hearing. A wonderful actress. After her death, it would be necessary to see that her surviving relations were well cared for; the state owed them—and her—that much.

An old man in a baggy suit came forward and spoke rhyming lines over the open grave. Some famous poet. Lowrey stifled a yawn. Behind the old poet stood two other men, each of whom clasped a shovel smartly in his hand. Lowrey wished the poet would shut up and give these two others a chance to work. A funeral was an event intended for putting a dead man's body into the earth where it wouldn't stink so bad. The rest of it—the posturing poetry, the endless chatter—could be dispensed with.

Beside him, the woman wept on. Hell, she was even moaning now. He needed someone to talk to. It was the only way he could rid himself of that haunting face he had seen an hour ago. So familiar, so unchanged by all the passing years. As he moved through the cemetery, past the mourning crowd, it had happened; the face appeared, smiling. For a brief moment, their eyes had actually met. Lowrey trembled at the memory. Durgas. Here. But why?

He wasn't sure he wanted to know. He scanned the other faces gathered beside the grave. He knew most of them; most were various cogs within the government. A few were foreigners, here as representatives of their governments, but he had allowed only the most important of these—the German ambassador, the president of the Soviet Union, the second secretary of the Chinese Communist party—to stand right up close to the grave, near enough so that they could see inside. Behind the circle of dignitaries, a vast swirling sea of faces stood. One must be Durgas, he knew. Unless he had run. But, no, Lowrey did not think he had run. There had been a lot in Durgas's face, much of it not readily decipherable, but fear had not been present. And Durgas may have been right not to be afraid. So far Lowrey had not raised an alarm. He had told no one of what he had seen—not even Rice, who had been walking only a few paces behind.

The poet concluded his recitation. Then came the abrupt,

shattering sound of dirt striking wood. Lowrey sighed with relief. In the distance, a band was playing "Yankee Doodle."

Lowrey studied the grave while the gravediggers worked, their shovels rising and falling in a coarse, rhythmic pattern. Good-bye, Tommy, he thought. And, with sincerity, he added, I'm sorry everything had to happen the way it did.

He turned away from the grave, drawing the woman with him. Together, they moved through a wave of extended hands. Lowrey shook a few, then waited for his bodyguards to clear a path to the car. A bird was singing, oblivious to the grief surrounding it. The woman wept on.

He allowed the woman to enter the car first, then followed. The door was closed from outside. Ahead, another path was being cleared, this one wide enough for the car to pass through. A man slipped into the front side beside the driver. John Rice.

Lowery turned to the woman and patted her knee. "You did just fine."

He told the driver, a middle-aged Negro he had known since Arkansas, "Go straight ahead, Cal, and wait on the highway for the rest of them to catch up with us. Once we get into the city, I want you to run this thing as fast as she'll go without making us look like we're in a hurry."

Cal said he could do that; the woman reached under her veil and stroked her eyes. The car bolted forward, pitching unsteadily like a boat in a storm.

Lowrey snapped, "Get your damn hands out of there. Put them in your lap."

"I'm not doing anything," the woman said. "Nobody can see me." This was her real voice, ugly and whiny, a far cry from Rachel's cool aristocratic tones.

"If you're going to play at being Rachel Bloome," Lowrey said, "then you better do it right. Rachel lost her husband today. You do what I tell you. Who the hell are you anyway?"

"My name is Ingrid Norton," she said.

"The general's daughter," Rice explained from the front.

"You mean we don't get to shoot her?" Lowrey said.

"I don't think that would be wise, Arnold."

"Hell. I thought she was an actress."

"I am," the girl said.

"Well, you better act good enough not to open your trap about this to anyone. And I mean your daddy too."

"I know that."

"I count ten cars in back of us, Mr. Lowrey," the driver reported. The car had stopped at the side of a wide highway.

"That's plenty, Cal. Let's roll."

There was another crowd here standing two-deep along both shoulders. Lowrey tried to ignore them. Durgas, Durgas, he was thinking.

"Is it something important, John?" Lowrey asked when the car had reached an open stretch of highway.

"I want to talk about the Russian thing," Rice said.

"What have you got?"

"Confirmation. A photograph. It's incredible. When you see it, you won't believe it."

"Probably not. I saw something myself today that was hard to believe. John Durgas—at the funeral."

"Oh, Jesus," Rice said.

"Hey, you're supposed to be crying," Lowrey reminded Ingrid Norton.

"How come?" She waved at the roadside. "Nobody can see me way out here."

"I can see you. Rachel killed herself this morning. The way I see it, somebody ought to cry for her. I can't. She hated my guts and I intend to respect that feeling. You cry—you ain't busy."

"This bomb," said Rice, "gives them an incredible edge over us. I hate to say this, Arnold, but I'm really scared. Ever since we received the first rumors, I've been talking to our best scientific people. They all said the same thing. Such a device was definitely a theoretical possibility. One was surprised the Germans hadn't come up with it years ago. Well, now it's a good deal more than theory. One scientist told me straight out—to my face—that I was a fool. He had been recommending just such a project for more than five years. I checked the records. He was right. Except the recommendations never reached me. Somebody shot them down way before they got that far."

"Some idiot," Lowrey said. "Make sure you have his head."

"That won't save us."

"Maybe not. But if we're lucky, Adolph will get his own bomb and go after them. They'll blow themselves to smithereens with their cosmic bombs and rockets. We'll go in and pick up the pieces."

"That didn't work last time, Arnold."

"Yeah. I know," Lowrey said softly.

"And this bomb is only a small, early model. I'm told in a year, two years, they should have a bomb big enough to wipe all of Washington clear off the map. One bomb, Arnold. They could smuggle it into New York Harbor, set it off, then— *bam*—Manhattan Island sinks into the sea."

"I've considered doing that myself a couple times."

"I'm not joking, Arnold."

"Me neither. I hate this fucking world. Is there anything to life except bigger bombs, newer guns, cosmic missiles. Wake up Tommy Bloome. I want to give him his country back again. What now? Do we start making our own bombs?"

"I've ordered the immediate creation of such a project. It'll take three years at least, depending on how much stuff my boys can steal from the Russians. I tell you I'm scared shitless. What about Durgas? You sure it was him you saw? This is really a hell of a day."

Lowrey was gazing out the side window. They had reached the center of the city now, proceeding down Tommy Bloome Boulevard at a fast but dignified clip. Thousands upon thousands of peering curious faces lined the walks, spilling into the roadway itself, streaming careless faces, each fading immediately into the next. Lowrey noticed the absence of smiles here but also the absence of tears. He waved at the crowd, receiving no response for his effort. Beside him, Ingrid Norton was weeping hopelessly.

"Yeah, it was him," he told Rice. Then he explained the circumstances surrounding his recognition of Durgas in the crowd.

"It's hard to believe. He's stayed away this long. Why should he come back now? Durgas wasn't sentimental, was he?"

Lowrey laughed sharply. "I tell you I saw him."

"I'm not doubting your word. But several dozen men, men who ought to know Durgas, walked past that same spot. Including me. Why didn't any of us see him?"

"You weren't looking. I was."

"Bob Ennis is here too. Did you see him?"

Lowrey recognized that the subject had been changed. But that was all right. Outside, in the crowd, an old woman was furiously waving a bright-red flag. Here was a raging fist fight. Lowrey ordered Cal to stop the car. Leaning past the sobbing woman, he watched the progress of the fight. A mass of flying angry fists sliced through the air. A cop appeared on horseback. His nightstick rose, sailed, fell. *Thump*. The mob splintered.

"Go on," Lowrey told Cal. Then, to Rice, "Kill him."

"Immediately?"

"Yes. It was him who killed Rachel."

"In public?"

"Christ, no. We're in no position to start popping off people in the streets. Especially now with Tommy gone. Wait until dark. Catch him alone and plug him. Burn the body."

The car halted in front of the Tower. Lowrey waited until his bodyguards, traveling in the car behind, disembarked and assumed their usual positions. Then, stepping into the open air, Lowrey headed toward home.

"I'd like you to come over to my office," Rice said, following.

"Now?"

"I'd prefer it. There'll be scientists there. And my military chiefs of staff. I think we ought to talk this thing out."

"All right, come on." For a man of his bulk, Lowrey moved lightly on his feet. Inside the Tower, safely sheltered by the high gray walls of the foyer, he relaxed. He ordered one guard to lock the front door, then stationed two additional men beside it. Ingrid Norton had accompanied them inside. Lowrey tore the veil off her face. She was young and pretty, with large pronounced lips and a hard jaw.

"You can go," Lowrey said. "I wanted to see if you looked like Rachel."

"Not in the least," she said, as if this were a matter of personal pride.

"I said get away from me."

When she was gone, Lowrey, Rice, and two bodyguards rode an elevator to the basement and, from there, went immediately into the passageway that led beneath the courtyard to the adjoining basement of the FBI building. They passed directly underneath the spot where the red brick wall had once stood.

Rice's private office was filled with several dozen dignified, pipe-smoking, shabbily dressed men. There was also a sprinkling of military officers. Lowrey dropped into a vacant chair and motioned Rice down beside him. When the briefing began, Lowrey listened intently to every third word. He heard: atoms, nuclei, chain reaction, fission. An army general mentioned uranium. Another man said it was an isotope. Craters were discussed. Five miles in diameter? Or ten?

At the end, standing, he authorized the immediate creation of a crash project designed to build and explode an atomic bomb in the least possible time. Someone in the back burst into excited applause.

After the others had gone, Lowrey told Rice, "I'm exhausted. First thing in the morning, call and tell me about Ennis."

"He'll be dead."

"I hope so."

"And Durgas?" asked Rice. "What about him?"

"I don't know," Lowrey said. "Maybe it wasn't Durgas, after all."

"In any event I'll look into it."

"Yes, do that."

In the corridor, Lowrey was joined by his bodyguards. It was late—past ten. Back in the Tower, he took an elevator to his quarters on the top floor, the fourteenth. He stationed guards near the entrance to his apartment, then went inside and bolted the door at his back.

One light was always kept burning. He turned on another and inspected the living room. He threw his jacket at a couch, missed, kicked off his shoes, and padded toward the bedroom. The apartment had been designed especially for his use, but he thought it a cold and lifeless place and avoided these gray walls except for sleep.

Opening the bedroom door, he turned on the light.

Stepping inside, looking straight ahead, he saw Durgas, who sat on the edge of the big canopied bed. Their eyes met.

"Arnold," said Durgas. "How have you been?"

Lowrey shut the door softly, suppressing his fear, fighting the desire to shiver and weep. His hands were trembling uncontrollably. He shoved them deep in his pockets. "Fine," he said, barely managing a whisper, "just fine."

Chapter Thirteen

Directly ahead of him, standing so that her untidy bulk blocked his view, stood a fat lady, done up in her holiday best. Beyond her, there was nothing but the thick single strand of the rope barrier and the mounted cop. Ennis decided to risk a scene. He dug an elbow into the lady's back, stepped back while she jumped, then squeezed through. He leaned far across the rope, peering down the long boulevard, and caught a distant glimpse of the receding line of black limousines. The first of the cars, the one in which Tommy Bloome's coffin rested, was barely in sight. Still, Ennis continued to stare until the last car had disappeared wholly from view. Then he stepped back and allowed the fat lady to reclaim her former spot. In a hurt voice she said, "You could have asked," but he was wondering, What is all this? here he had come more than three thousand miles, forsaking his last chance at continued life, and for what? What had he seen so far? An open limousine. A hired driver. A seat piled high with paper flowers. A plain, unadorned wooden box. And then cars, more cars. In one, Rachel and Lowrey. In the rest, strangers. What did all of it mean? Anything? Tommy was dead: that was the one significant fact he could discern.

Now he tried to get away from the crowd. As he turned, a passing band began to blare. He shoved a body out of his path, eager now to get away. "Sorry—bathroom," he murmured. Like Tommy, he loathed crowds. Too many people in one place at one time—it brought out the very worst in the human race. The mob was packed all the way from the edge of the road to the storefronts behind. Ennis managed to fight his way to one of the stores and tried the doorknob but it was locked tight. Glancing into the crowd, he saw the men coming after him. He had spotted them this morning at the airport, only two men. They were no longer trying to conceal

155

themselves from him. Ennis waved. They came hurrying after.

He struggled back into the crowd, moving parallel to the street. Eventually he reached a corner and turned down a side street. Almost at once the crowd began to thin. Soon enough he was walking on open pavement. Behind, he could still hear the band—or another one—playing "America the Beautiful" now. The two men came out of the crowd. Ennis ignored them and sat down upon a sidewalk bench. The two men apparently did not intend to arrest him yet; plainly they had been given no order to shoot on sight. He didn't think it was worth the effort to try to shake them. Besides, he was convinced these men were not the only ones following him. There were probably others—in the shadows.

So, right now, he didn't intend moving unless somebody came up and made him. He had originally intended to visit the grave site, but that no longer seemed wise or necessary. He had attended Tommy's funeral, if only a tiny portion of it, and that was all he had wanted. He was here in Washington. That was victory enough. Having known Tommy in life, it was not essential that he also know him in death.

A young girl walked past; she couldn't have been more than eighteen at the most, tears streaming awkwardly down flushed cheeks. She was a pretty girl, though not beautiful, with a pale, bony face and big eyes. Her dress was old, patched, and much too brief. He wondered if she was crying for Tommy—or was it a more personal matter? Most likely she had just had a silly fight with her boyfriend. Should he go forward and ask? But fifty-year-old men did not go around asking personal questions of good-looking young girls. Not in strange cities, and Washington, despite the two years he had lived and worked here, was a strange and alien place to him. He looked again, but the girl had disappeared. A bright sign caught his eye. FOOD.

Getting up, he did not need to look behind. He knew the men were back there. The music had ceased; the band had gone past. Except for a few gently chattering pedestrians, the street was silent and deserted. The restaurant was partway to the corner. He hurried, the odor of cooking food beckoning him forward. He hadn't eaten a bite in more than a day.

"Say, mister."

He looked down. It was the girl, the one he had noticed. Although her eyes were red from tears, she had ceased crying.

"Do you have any money on you?" she asked.

"Money. Yes. I— What do you want it for?"

"I saw you looking at me. I thought—well, I thought how I've got to eat something."

"In here?" He pointed at the restaurant.

"It's as good a place as any."

"Then come on."

Before leaving the shadows of the doorway, the girl looked carefully up and down the street, then followed him quickly inside. It was a tiny cramped place. The menu above the counter proclaimed that the special of the day, hamburger steak, could be had for eighty-five cents. Ennis pointed to an unoccupied booth at the back of the diner. He and the girl went that way and sat, facing each other.

"Do you know what you want?" he asked her.

"It depends on how much money you have."

"More than enough."

"Well, you see," she said, "that's another problem. When I get through eating here, then I'm still going to be broke." She laughed brightly, as if Ennis had reached over and tickled her. "Fat but poor. That means tonight I'll just have to ask somebody else. Another man," she added enthusiastically.

"I'll give you whatever you need," he said. Talking with her had succeeded not only in reviving him but, in a way, actually saving him. "When we're done. But there's something I want to ask you first."

"Oh, yeah?" For the first time he noticed she was chewing gum. "What's that?"

"When I saw you. When you were crying. Well, what was it for? Was it the funeral?"

"Funeral?"

"Tommy Bloome's funeral," he said with impatience.

"Oh, yeah. I heard he died." She laughed with real pleasure. "I wasn't crying for him. Why should I cry for him? I never knew him. That's funny, thinking I was crying for him."

"Then why were you crying?"

"A cop was bothering me. I was crying to make him let me alone. Some old woman back there set him on me. Claimed I was trying to steal her purse."

"So you didn't care about Tommy?"

"Not a bit," she said brightly. "He was a real asshole."

"A what?" said Ennis, more appalled than he cared to reveal. "Tommy was what?"

The girl spoke distinctly. "A real asshole. People starving to death all over the country, getting sent out to Nevada to die in the desert. And where's this hero all the time? This great guy Tommy? He's in Africa, or he's in China, or maybe in Russia. What do they need him for? If he was so tremendous, why didn't he stay here and help us? My mother said, when he was in Washington, they used to have to wash down the streets every morning because they were covered with blood. He killed thousands, she said."

"Maybe he had enemies," Ennis said, fighting to stay calm.

She treated his words as a joke and smiled appreciatively. "You bet he did. He sure didn't have many friends."

"Can you remember the Depression?" He felt it was imperative she be made to comprehend the situation of ten years ago.

"Why should I? Can't you starve to death just as easy now as you could back then?"

The waitress shuffled into view, bearing a pair of soiled waterglasses. Ennis ordered the hamburger steak and the girl did too. As the waitress turned away, the girl swiveled slightly and swept the room with a careful glance.

"Friends of yours?" she asked, nodding furtively toward the counter.

"They're following me," Ennis said.

"Cops?"

"FBI, I think."

She giggled. "Oh, crap."

"No." For some reason he felt defensive. "They are. You don't know who I am."

The girl appeared to consider. Abruptly she stood up. "If you're somebody that bad, I think maybe I better get out of here. I'm not that hungry."

Ennis grabbed her arm. "No, please. Don't go."

"Sure." She sat down with a plop and, raising both hands high over her head, stretched luxuriously.

"Explain what you meant," he said. "About starving."

"Don't you know?"

He shook his head. "I'm from the West Coast."

"Can't you starve out there?"

"I never did."

"Well, lucky for you. But, look here, if it's what you want, I can just tell you my story. I'm Laura Elder. What's your name?"

"Bob Dixon." But, regretting the lie immediately, he said, "Bob Ennis."

"Two names?" She laughed. "Maybe they *are* FBI. But I was going to tell you my story. It really starts two years ago. My father is dead and I'm living with Mother. She's a seamstress. They shipped him to Mojave when I was eight and he never came back. Mom worked in a little dress shop run by this fantastically old lady who had had the place since way before the revolution. At first, since she was so old, they said she could keep it, but she wouldn't die off like they wanted, so finally they gave the word they were closing the place and everybody would have to move downtown to a big factory. Except they didn't have enough places for everyone. In the factory, that is. So my mother and these two other ladies were out. Tough. She went to the employment office first thing the next morning. She kept going every morning but there was nothing. She was forty and had never done nothing in her life except sew and they had machines to do that. I was still going to school. Mom was scared—she knew after a month out of work you're immediately classified as Excess Labor—and she started talking about running away to Canada. Crazy stuff. She kept saying how Dad was up there, but I knew he was just dead. Well, anyway, pretty soon the month was up and they didn't wait a minute. She got her notice: a reclamation project in Las Vegas, something to do with Boulder Dam. Then she really got scared and said she'd never go. I knew she would. She wasn't the type to fight and neither was I. So I ran away that same night. I lived with a friend for six months, hiding in the basement. That got boring. I took off and found another place. I've been going ever since. I even lived with one of the district commissioners one time for a month till he got scared and threw me out in the snow."

"So you don't live anywhere?" Ennis said. "You just live by begging?"

"I hope the hell not," she said, pretending to be offended. "I'm what you call between situations now. But I can always find a place to sleep. Some things never fail me."

"How old are you?"

"Twenty," she said casually.

"No, you're not."

"O.K., then how does thirteen sound? Or forty? Or a hundred and ninety-nine? What's it to you?"

By this time the waitress had long since brought their meals. Laura had finished hers, eating between sentences, but Ennis wasn't hungry. He pushed his plate across the table. "You can eat it."

"Thanks." She started right in. "This isn't half-bad."

Leaning back in the booth, Ennis waited for her to be done. The men at the counter drank their coffee in silence. The diner was nearly empty now. He guessed the parade must be over.

When Laura finished eating, she folded her hands primly in her lap and said. "Now about that money . . ."

He stood up. "Let's go."

"Wait." She shook her head. "What do you have in mind?"

"I thought we'd just walk around. And talk. Do you mind?"

There was no need for her to mention the promised money. "It's too hot for walking. I'd die. Why don't you take me to a movie?"

"We couldn't talk there."

"Is that what you have in mind?" Her cynical smile blossomed.

"Yes," he said curtly. "But come on, we'll go to a movie."

They went out. Ennis stopped to pay, shielding the contents of his wallet from her prying gaze. He had less than ten dollars; he didn't want her to know.

The street outside was silent, nearly deserted. The few people in sight, lounging against various storefronts, were old men, dirty, tattered—bums and beggars. The girl directed him toward Tommy Bloome Boulevard. They crossed that wide street and continued straight ahead. There was a movie theater two blocks farther down.

The program was a double feature, a western and an action story set in the East African revolution. They found seats in the crowded balcony. Laura grabbed his hand and wouldn't let go. The East African film was showing. For a moment Ennis concentrated upon the bright, full-color carnage: German soldiers blown to bits by revolutionary cadres. Laura never said a word; the pressure of her hand on his did not deviate. The newsreel was about Tommy. Intrigued in spite of himself, Ennis watched with interest. The film began with a history of Tommy's career told through the means of old still photographs and an occasional newsreel clip. During one segment, the inaugural ceremonies of 1935, Ennis saw himself standing at Tommy's side. The girl did not appear to recognize him. Halfway through the newsreel she left to buy popcorn. He gave her two dimes. Tommy lay in his coffin. Mourners moved past. The widow wept copious tears and spoke of her grief. The film concluded with Arnold Lowrey reading a brief message concerned with the passing of his "best and truest friend and comrade, a gentleman in the fullest American sense of the term." Lowrey appeared to be weeping. Ennis felt sick at his stomach.

After this the western began. The girl hurriedly reclaimed her seat, passing Ennis one of two bags of dry popcorn. He refused, telling her to eat both. On the screen a tribe of red Indians was savagely murdering a family of white settlers.

By the time they left the theater it was late. Getting dark. Too late to go to the park—anywhere—too late to talk. The girl would demand her money now and he would hand it over and she would leave. There was no way he could stop her.

But she never mentioned the money. Outside the theater she grabbed his sleeve and pointed down a narrow alley. "This way."

"What's there?"

"Some people I know."

"What's the idea?"

Her smiled disarmed him. She shook her head. "You wanted to talk. I can't stay out after dark. No papers."

"Me neither," he said.

"So, come on."

He hesitated, sensing a trap, but why would she want to do that? Hadn't he already promised her his money? What else could he give?

"O.K.," he said.

They moved down the dark lane past the squat, hunched relics of old apartment buildings. At the end the girl, glancing behind, turned left, leading him back into the sun. She proceeded along this street for half a block, then suddenly leaped across the gutter and sprang across the street. Ennis ran too.

She skipped up the steps of a red brick apartment building and opened the door. She waited for him to join her, then stepped into a dark lobby. They crossed a frayed carpet, then up a winding flight of stairs—three floors—and down a short corridor.

"Is this the place?" he asked. "Your friends live—"

"Hush," she whispered. "I'm trying to ditch them."

"Who?"

"Your FBI pals. We can't take them where we're going."

"I'd almost forgotten them."

"They were sitting right behind us in the movie."

He shook his head. "I didn't look."

Along the hall she went from door to door, trying each knob. Finally one opened and she waved. "In here, quick."

She locked the door behind him, leaned over, kissed him on the cheek. "Safe," she said. "Now go and look out the window. Unless I got mixed up, you should be able to see the street. And watch out."

Ennis went to the window and pulled back a torn shade. Through a thin wispy drapery he gazed down into the street. He hadn't noticed before, but the street was teeming with unexpected life. Opposite, nearly every porch contained a group of talking, gesturing men of various ages. While he watched, several women strolled past. At the corner a knot of children played hopscotch—young girls—and he saw young lean legs flashing white as brief girlish skirts flapped in the wind.

"I can see one of them," he told Laura. "Across the street."

"The other's probably in the building," she said. "Now keep quiet."

"Won't they search for us?"

"They'd need a lot of extra men for that. There's fifty or sixty apartments in a building this size."

"They might not want to cause that much trouble."

"Then maybe we're safe," she said.

For the first time he had a chance to survey the apartment. This room was quite bare. "How did you know you'd find an open door?"

She shrugged. "There's usually a couple in every building in this neighborhood. Where do you think I sleep at night? A lot of managers know about people like me and help out."

"But—" he started.

She put a finger over her lips and went into the next room. There was a small bathroom as well, but no kitchen. He followed her into the second room, nearly identical to the first. Across the bottom of one wall in bright childish crayon someone had scrawled, Bobby—June 15 1947. In both rooms the only source of light was a bare overhead bulb in the ceiling. Laura saw him looking at the switch and said, "Better leave it off."

He nodded.

Then she removed her dress. It came over her head like a curtain rising to reveal a play. Underneath, she wore nothing.

"Don't," he said.

She placed her dress upon the floor, spreading the garment so that it covered the maximum possible space. "I know the facilities aren't plush," she said, "but it's the best I can offer."

"You don't understand," he said, feeling guilty over the lack of money in his wallet. "Look—"

She sat down upon the dress and crossed her legs. She folded her slender arms underneath small breasts. "I had a baby one time," she said, indicating the red creases upon her abdomen. "You don't mind?"

"Why should I?"

"Then why tell me no?"

"What if they came in here and found us?"

"Then we'd have to hurry to get off before they got the cuffs on us." She stretched her arms out toward him, smiling in her faintly mocking way, a duplication of the fading smiles of a hundred Hollywood queens. "Come on."

He took off his clothes. Removing his pants, he held out his wallet and said, "Take it now—I promised you."

She shook her head. "Not now—later." She rolled over on her back and parted her things lewdly.

He took her easily, quickly, too quickly. At one point he thought he heard what might have been an insistent tapping upon a distant door. He tried to move with the girl, with Laura, matching his motions to hers. But it had been too long a time.

Rolling away, Laura used a portion of the dress to wipe her thighs, then stood up. Transforming her slender hands into tiny fists, she threw them high over her head and stretched on tiptoed feet, reaching toward the ceiling. She smiled at him, shook her head to indicate there were no words, then went to the window. He saw her backside for the first time. There was a jaunty impish innocence to this part of her, a youthful prancing motion to her buttocks, soft smooth boyish flanks of pale flesh that had somehow managed to avoid the rapid coarsening that had infected her more exposed forward half. Bending down, spine wrinkling under her skin, she peered through the draperies.

"Nothing. But it's dark now and they don't light these streets very well." She turned and showed him her hands. "They may be hiding."

"Who cares?" He fought against a strange feeling of despondency, almost despair.

"The man I'm taking you to—he cares."

"Who's he?"

"A guy who can help you." She moved away from the window, her features nearly invisible in the dark.

"How?"

"However you want. If you're really in trouble, he can sneak you out of the country. Or hide you."

"Then you do know who I am?"

"Nope. And I don't want to know either. I've even forgotten your name—your last name anyway. I try to stay away from this underground stuff. A person could get killed."

"Underground? What are you talking about?"

"You know. Shooting cops. Blowing up buildings. Bombing trains. How do I know what you did? And I don't want to know either, so don't tell me." She covered her ears dramatically and made a frightened face.

"Look," he said, understanding the futility of this, the absurd mistake. "You've got me wrong. I don't want you to take me anywhere. Get the money and go. I'm sorry there isn't very much. I guess you must have thought—"

"Stuff your money. I'm not a whore."

"I never said you were." The darkness had increased. He stood beside her now, sensing her presence more than seeing it.

"Stuff your money anyway."

"Look." He took her cold rigid hand, finding it with difficulty. Then he touched the gentle flesh of her rear. "I don't know why you want to help me, but I'm glad. Really. You've made me happy today. But nobody can save me. Those men are still out there. I'm sure of it. They aren't going to let me go."

"Are you that important?" she asked.

"Yes," he said. He went to the window and looked out. The only light came from a dim streetlamp far down at the end of the block. He could see the children down there still, hopping, jumping, playing their infinite game. Across the street, beyond the flat roofs of the opposite buildings, he could see the high bright summit of the Tower. Squinting, he tried to see if the lights were burning on the top floor. Was Lowrey home tonight? Was Rachel with him?

He returned to the girl, finding her standing in the dark, and knelt down, turning her legs slightly, and kissed her upon the rump. Too exhausted to stand, he remained on his knees.

"Just go," he said. "Please. I'm on the wrong side. I was Tommy Bloome's friend, his best."

She did not answer.

"It's true. I lived with him for the last eight years of his life. In Washington state. Beside the ocean. Just the two of us. Now they want to kill me too. And they will. I don't care. Understand?"

She slipped away from him, transformed into a white, ghostly wraith that swooped and darted through the room with endless grace and precision. Suddenly she stood beside him, fully dressed.

"I could still help you. I mean that."

"No," he said. "I'm ready to die."

"That's stupid."

"Maybe it is."

She left him, her dress rustling softly. A faint light reached him when the front door opened, but that was all. He knew he ought to go and turn the lock, but the effort was presently beyond him.

What kind of day had this been? Today? His last day? Kneeling naked in this dank and empty room, breathing this dust-choked air, he felt a sudden need to somehow assess and comprehend these final hours of life, to consolidate the whole into an entity both meaningful and complete. But he could not do it; he tried and nothing seemed to work. From the girl—with Laura—he had intended to discover this other world, the one he and Tommy had created but never been allowed to know. But the girl had proved to be ridden by contradictions; she had been, in the end, impossible, as uncertain as a reflection seen in a cracked mirror. Each time he'd thought he knew her, she had changed into someone else entirely, like one of those lizards sold in cheap dime stores, like a chameleon. First she had seemed to want his money and then to help him and finally she had lain upon the hardwood floor with her legs open. And now she had left his wallet. Intact. Yet another contradiction. She had been something new to him, a product of the revolution, a creature forged in the bowels of the factory he and Tommy had created. When the first shots were fired, she was four years old. Only four, but what was she now? How did she feel about this world she had been given? Could she comprehend the awfulness of the old? After a full day with the girl, he could not answer these questions. He could guess. Nothing more.

Dressing, he then made his way to the front room and passed boldly out the door. The corridor was empty. He found the stairway. Went down.

It was a hot, sweltering night, typical for Washington in July. A delicate wind stirred the air. At the corner the children continued to work at their game. The Tower hung above like a sleek second moon. He turned his back upon it and went another way.

Around him the city grew darker and more silent, as

though all life huddled near a central place and never dared to venture into these distant, forgotten avenues. Streetlamps were occasional reminders of a brighter past. He went for long blocks, seeing no light at all. Beyond the narrow sidewalks buildings were piled close together like boxes, their farthermost walls touching tenderly. He met no one, heard nothing. Not the empty yip of a dog. The casual howl of a cat. He was reminded of the forest around Neah Bay, where often at night he went for aimless walks. He saw things that way now: the buildings were trees, the sidewalk a path through the wilderness. The stars were above; that much had never changed.

He passed a bar. Against a wide dark window a cocktail glass glimmered, outlined clearly in blazing neon. He paused at the door and listened. Someone laughed. A pinball machine clicked and whirred. He almost went inside. But it wouldn't be right. He was an explorer, a pathfinder. He hurried away, fearful of confronting too much civilization too soon; the forest was his domain.

"Tommy Bloome is an asshole," he heard, echoing from behind. From where? The bar? He moved faster. The darkness of a primitive world swept over him. He plunged forward—into the heart of God.

Now, finally, he heard them coming. Their footsteps pounded behind. He stopped; they stopped. He started again; they started. Well, shoot; he thought. I'm alone. Nobody's going to see or hear or give a damn. Do your business, earn your pay. Kill—quickly.

"Stop," cried a voice.

Ennis ran. A hot wind swept through his tangled hair. He heard them chasing, their footsteps mingling, mixing with his own, and he sang along with the rhythm, beating a melody into the thunderous pounding of their percussive pursuing feet. He sang his song, howled his story, and spun around a corner, sliding on the flat heel of one shoe, smashing against a wooden fence, rebounding, flashing ahead, laughing now. Ennis ran for his life—pretending it was a thing that truly mattered to someone, had to be protected and saved, salvaged—the very act of doing so resounded inside him like a mighty YES, a cry of affirmative faith, of salvation.

The stars above suddenly brightened, flashing orange, red.

He saw the alley. Grinning, he left the sidewalk and threw himself down, crouching, waiting. He heard them coming, thought they must hear him too, the way he was breathing, but the stars had faded, the night was blacker than ever. The two men went past, shadows of the deepest black; they seemed to see nothing. They paused at the corner.

"I heard him—he went this way."

"No, down here."

"Then we lost him. I told you—"

"Dammit, I said here."

They were gone. Crouching at the lip of the alley, Ennis hugged his knees and shook with laughter. He had won! They were beaten, gone, lost. The stars themselves had come down to Earth to offer their bright salvation.

Looking up at the sky, he thought, Thank you, Tommy. God bless you.

For several minutes, he remained huddled where he was, listening calmly to his own distant heartbeat. When nothing happened, he rose to his feet and turned. Not toward the street. He went the other way, walking cautiously to the end of the alley.

A dim light burned here, showing him a bare wooden fence. He found a foothold, grabbed the top of the fence, caught a splinter in his palm, boosted himself up, swore at the pain, dropped soundlessly on the opposite side.

It was dark here. He could see nothing.

Tentatively he took a forward step.

A cat screeched. Something moved in the dark. The cat? A rat? Ennis lunged back, startled, and tripped, lost his balance, fell, smacked the fence hard with the back of his head. He lay in a trembling heap and heard the sound of laughter.

A light flared. A round yellow sun pecked at his eyelids. He forced himself to stare straight into the light.

"Hello there."

He recognized the voice immediately, knowing it as positively as if he had last heard it an hour ago, not ten years or more.

The light turned upon itself, briefly exposing the man's face. It was a confirmation Ennis did not require. The narrow face glowed ghostly pale, circled by the stark man-made light of the flashlight.

Ennis made himself whisper, "Durgas."

"Yes."

Once more the light shone upon the face.

Turning quickly, before the other could see and stop him, Ennis lifted a hand and waved at the stars—at Tommy. Then, turning back, he faced the light, awaiting the final moment of raw judgment and knowing it would not be long in coming. Durgas stepped toward him.

Chapter Fourteen

When Tommy Bloome left Washington midway through the bitter winter of 1940–41, as the train upon which he was the only passenger left the invisible boundaries of the District of Columbia and plunged into the frozen country of lower Maryland, he could not help feeling a deep sense of real relief. As the train continued north, skirting past Baltimore and then turning west, he attempted to analyze and understand his own feelings. During the month since the ouster vote, he had allowed himself only a single emotion: rage. Revenge and schemes of revenge had fully occupied his mind. But now—well, revenge didn't seen very important now. Lowrey and Durgas wanted the government. So let them have it. Perhaps they deserved it. Perhaps it deserved them too. Who was to say?

As the train slipped quietly into Ohio, Tommy remembered how he had at first refused to take their decision seriously. He had told them, "Gentlemen, I'm sorry but you have just signed your own death warrants. I swear that I'll have each and every goddamned one of you—and I'm including you too, Arnold—up against the brick wall by dawn tomorrow. There's no way you can rid yourselves of me. I am the revolution. Without me, you will not and cannot survive a single week. I am Tommy Bloome. And none of the rest of you can say that."

None of them could, no, but still, even though the facts could not be altered, they could at least be overcome. And that was what they had apparently managed to achieve. A month had passed and the revolutionary government remained intact and secure. Tommy knew a good part of this was his own doing. He had refused to fight them publicly. And they had won. Of them all, there was only one he truly hated and that was Durgas. And Durgas not because he had

worked to oust Tommy Bloome, not even because his
treachery had gone deeper than any (Tommy fully understood that it was Durgas who had instigated the revolt). No.
He hated Durgas for what he had done with Rachel, using
her madness as a weapon against her husband. This Tommy
would never forgive. By using her, Durgas had violated an
unwritten trust, a higher law than either of them could
write. Given an opportunity, even in his presently mellow
mood, he could have killed Durgas on the spot.

The train went only as far as Port Angeles, still a good
fifty miles east of his actual destination. A car met him there
and conveyed him the last winding miles along a badly paved
road overlooking the roaring white water channel of the
Strait of Juan de Fuca.

At Neah Bay, Bob Ennis was waiting. The settlement—a
general store, Indian agency, a small movie theater, and a
log townhall—seemed either asleep or dead. And it was
raining too. Ennis appeared, huddled beneath a wide um-
brella. The two of them raced through a slanting rain and
found shelter within the log hall. Ennis sat on a wooden
bench and wiped the rain off his face.

"Well, Tommy," he said. "Together again."

"How do you feel about it?"

Ennis shrugged. "It's all part of the past now, Tommy.
If I wanted to bear grudges, I could. But I didn't ask you
here for that."

Tommy nodded and sat beside his friend. "Now I know
how you must have felt, Bob. The shoe is on the other
foot—my foot. We ought to get along. We have that much
in common."

Ennis shook his head, as if wiping a slate clean. "No, Tommy. Don't look back. I never do. You—you can't."

These words were the nearest Ennis ever came to speaking
harshly to Tommy Bloome. For years afterward, they shared
a small cabin some five miles from the settlement. In 1936
Ennis had settled here. At night he often took long solitary
walks while Tommy remained in the cabin, rocking in a
chair, reading an occasional book, often just sitting and
staring. For the first few months Tommy looked upon his
life here at the edge of the continent as a new beginning, a
second start at life, but he soon had to admit that this could

never be. A man is allowed only one life which he must take and use as he wishes. Tommy had had his life; his preferred destiny was done now; his life lay behind him, finished and over. In other words, though he was hardly more than forty, he was a dead man in every sense but the most final: his soul remained intact within his physical form. One winter Tommy wrote his memoirs, composing nightly paragraphs in thick spiral notebooks. He threw the lot away when spring arrived at last. Another time, in the spring too, he suffered a brief but tumultuous love affair with a bronze-skinned native of indeterminate age. Her name was Jenny. On a few occasions, at Lowrey's request, he traveled to Washington; once he met Stalin. He fished a great deal too. There were creeks and streams nearby, many of them stocked with fat rainbow trout, and the Pacific Ocean, too, swarming with salmon. Ennis often hunted—deer mostly—but Tommy did not enjoy that sport. Every Saturday night, when the weather held, they walked the five miles to the settlement and watched a movie. The films were invariably dreadful, either mindless entertainment or blatant propaganda. Tommy shrugged. None of this was supposed to be life; it was only living.

On Sundays, rising late, past noon, he would lie in bed, drinking hot tea and reading the *National Times*. He enjoyed reading of his own exploits in distant faraway lands. He confessed to Ennis, who refused to glance at the paper, that these public stories assumed the place in his life of private daydreams. "I could never imagine any of this for myself, you see. Me—a revolutionary fighter in the Gobi Desert? Good God, Bob, I can't hit the trunk of a fat tree with a rifle at six inches. I won't even shoot a deer. I'm madly in love with life these days. And here I am"—he slapped the *Times*—"killing ten thousand Chinese warlords a week with my bare hands. It's a hell of a life, you know."

Ennis must have known, though he never told Tommy. They seldom spoke, both knowing it was wisest to limit their conversation, for neither man had anyone else and it would not make sense—living so close—to grow bored with each other too soon. For Tommy, the thoughts he felt most strongly were concerned with a subject he could never openly discuss with Ennis. Tommy carried within him an inner life that dominated everything that existed outside. His cache of secrets was immense and never to be revealed.

He did tell Ennis one time—this was late in 1944—that he was satisfied. "I have lived a full life. I don't imagine any man has ever come as close as I have to realizing all his dreams and ambitions. For me, there was never more than the one dream. I don't know, maybe it was less a dream and more a nightmare. I dreamed I saw a world ruled over by a tiny grotesque elite of evil men, maddened by their own overwhelming power, grown rich and fat while beneath their feet millions starved for the simple necessities of life. I saw a vast army of these men sweeping across the globe, enveloping land after land, people after people. I saw a whole world living in constant dreadful fear, trembling beneath the upraised boot of a dark and unseen god. That was my dream, my nightmare, and I vowed that it would not happen here. And I succeeded. Perhaps not so completely as I might have wished. The war I sought with Germany—and certainly the Nazis are creatures come to life from my nightmare world—was kept from me. But I did save my own country, my own people. Our system is not a perfect one. It is ruled by men and the men are far from perfect themselves. My own hands are stained with the blood of thousands, many of them guilty, yes, but there were innocent ones too and they are no less dead than the guilty. But I say that I am satisfied. And I am proud. I made my dream real."

Aside from Bob Ennis, Tommy's only real friend in Neah Bay was an ancient Indian known as Tyee John. John ran a small fishing boat out of Neah Bay, and he and Tommy often went out together into the wild Pacific waters beyond the cape. Out there, the turbulent waters rocking the fragile craft, Tommy felt a great sense of inner peace, a feeling of true serenity related not so much to a oneness with nature as to an awareness of aloneness within the self.

Tyee John said he'd never heard of Tommy Bloome before. He was his own boss. The revolution had not touched him at all, that was a white man's game.

Out on the ocean, the tiny boat jerking and rolling, then sliding softly forward upon a tall white wave, Tommy and John would talk. Behind the boat, two long lines cut invisibly through the waters.

"John," said Tommy. "Tell me something. Do you believe a man can live more than once? That once he dies, he can live again afterward?"

John gave the concept his total consideration. He said, "Do you mean heaven, Tommy?"

"No, not that. I suppose you might call it reincarnation, except that it happens this way: you die one year, say it was this year, it was 1943. Except that you are immediately born again, but when you are, in this new world you enter, it is 1923 again, the year when you were born in the first place. Except that you aren't a baby this time; you're as old as you were when you died. Do you see?"

"I see," said John, "but, no, I do not believe that can happen. I am a Christian and accept the Christian God. I am a Roman Catholic, as was my father before me. I do not go to church because I can see God more plainly out here than within the walls of a building. Look, Tommy—see him?— right there, over the bow of the boat. See him hovering up there in the middle of the air? See how he shines big like a great yellow light." John laughed, so it was not possible to tell if he was serious in his vision. "No, Tommy, I do not believe what you ask is possible."

"But what if it happened?"

"Did it?"

"Yes," Tommy said. "It happened to me. Exactly as I told you."

"Are you certain?" John asked.

"Would I make a mistake about something like that? I died—I was shot to death—in the year 1947. When I woke up, it was 1923, the day I had been born. This actually happened to me, John, and everything I have done since, I have done because of that. Because the world in which I died the first time was a horrible place and I have devoted my whole life—my second life—to making sure it couldn't happen here. And it hasn't. Because of me, this world is different from the one where I lived before. I have taken history and turned it around."

"I see," said John.

"It happened," Tommy said weakly.

"Then, if you say so, then, yes, I believe you. I say all things are possible. Why shouldn't this happen as well? Perhaps God in his wisdom felt you were a good man, that your death in that other time was wrong, so he granted you a second life. You tell me you have used your new life wisely, and I say that is right. What you say, I have never heard of it happening, but that does not signify that it cannot happen. If you say it is true, then I believe you, Tommy."

"It is true."

"Look—your line. You have a fish, Tommy."

Another afternoon, when he and John were bringing their boat back to the settlement after a long day's fishing, Tommy happened to glance across the water and there at the end of the pier stood an unfamiliar figure waving at him. This was during the spring or autumn of 1945. As the boat drew near, Tommy saw that the figure was a woman.

"Who is that?" he asked John. "It can't be Jenny."

"No. Not Jenny. A white woman."

"I can't tell," Tommy said, shading his eyes.

"She is dressed very well," said John.

The boat drew closer to the pier, gently bobbing in the calmer waters of the Bay. "I know her," Tommy said now. "It's Rachel, my wife."

"Does Jenny know of your wife?" John asked with a blank face.

"She's not really my wife. We separated many years ago when she turned against me."

"She is a very handsome person," John said, gazing across the water.

Climbing unsteadily from the boat, Tommy had no time to prepare himself before Rachel came rushing forward. She caught him in her arms and held him as if she never intended to let go. She said, "Tommy, I made them let me come. Oh, Tommy." Her lips brushed his; he felt her fingernails tearing at the thin fabric of his shirt.

Then he pushed her away.

She almost fell. But John, who had preceded Tommy off the boat, held her steady. She swayed precariously, then stood stiffly upright. John let her go. "It can be very slippery here," he said.

"Where can we talk?" Rachel asked Tommy.

"John, get out of here," Tommy said.

"I want to get my catch."

Tommy tried to calm himself. "Would you mind letting it wait?"

"No." John went back into the boat and brought out his salmon.

Tommy waited until he was safely out of earshot, then said, "Who let you come here?"

"Who do you think? I told him I had to see you and—"

"He was wrong. He promised me nobody was ever to come here unless I asked to see them."

"Tommy," she said, "do you care?"

"Yes."

"But"—she made a tentative effort at smiling—"I'm well. Can't you see? I'm cured. They released me from the hospital last month. It took almost forever for me to get Lowrey to say yes. I would have written, but he said you didn't accept mail. So I came this way. I want to stay with you. I'll do anything you ask, anything you want, anything at all. I think we ought to try to make it the same as it used to be. Remember? San Francisco? Oh, Tommy, please."

He heard her out without shifting the blankness of his expression. Then he said, "No."

He tried to step past her. She reached out and grabbed his arm. Her fingers, trembling, held his sleeve without particular force.

"Why?" she whispered. "Can't you see that I—I'm sorry for what happened. I am. I mean it. I wish I could say something more. I was sick. They used me. I didn't know what I was doing. You can't blame me for that, can you?"

"Yes, I can," he said, drawing away from her at last. "And I do." He went quickly along the pier. The wet planks quivered beneath his feet. He reached the end, then heard her coming from behind. *Squeek, squeek,* said the planks.

He waited, then suddenly turned. His open hand waved a wide circle. He caught her across the face, backhanded. She toppled right down. Her lower lip, split at the center, was bleeding.

"I don't want to see you here again," he said. "I mean never. If you try to come back, I swear I'll kill you with these." Bending down, he held his hands close to her face, actually touching her torn lip with the knuckles. "See?"

He wiped the blood off on his shirt front.

He waited for her to cry. He expected her to beg. When she didn't, when she remained silent, he turned and went away. He walked straight home to the cabin, and when he came through the front door, Ennis, who had been washing dishes in the kitchen, ran out and cried, "Rachel was here."

"Yes, I know. I met her on the dock."

"Is she staying?"

"No."

"Has she gone?"

"Yes."

Besides Rachel, in all the time he lived at the cabin, Tommy admitted only one other visitor from the outside. Lowrey never knew about this visit. Had he known, he would have been greatly disturbed; he might have been frightened half to death.

The time was summer, the first week of July, 1946. The air was hot, still, and humid. The ocean breeze that normally circulated here was absent this day. Tommy spent the afternoon in the cabin, reading a part of a life of Flaubert. Oddly, while he seldom enjoyed reading novels, the men who wrote them fascinated him as individuals. He thought the best of writers were really politicians in disguise, men who rid themselves of an inner craving for power by manipulating unreal people upon a printed page rather than taking the risk of attempting the same tactics with real flesh-and-blood people in the real dirt-and-grass world.

Even after the sun set, the air did not cool off. Tommy sat with the windows in the cabin open wide. Ennis came in from the kitchen and said, "It's time for my walk."

"You're not going anywhere in particular?"

"I thought I'd stop by the settlement. I'm expecting some magazines in the mail."

"If you see John, tell him I want to go out on the water tomorrow. It ought to be cool there."

"Anything else?"

Tommy said no.

"Then I'll see you in a while."

As soon as he was alone, Tommy laid his book aside and went to the nearest window, looking out. Because of the huddling trees that stood like sentries around the front of the cabin, it was difficult to see the sky. In spite of the heat, he was not wholly uncomfortable. In a way, now that he was alone, he felt almost cool, actually relaxed. He thought it was largely his own sense of satisfaction that permitted him to feel this way. More and more, lately—and it had been almost six years now—he had been able to forget the bitterness of his ouster and remember instead the tremendous pride he now felt for all the grand accomplishments of his life. In a way he was anticipating his own death, for he expected it to come any time now. He felt he could die without caring, without regret. There was nothing more either to be done or undone. He was finished. And, thinking this, he smiled at the dark rectangle of the open window. The sweet clean still air reached his nostrils. He sighed. He stood at the window a considerable time, thinking, smelling, not dreaming. Just remembering. And waiting.

Then he heard a knock upon the door.

For a moment he was genuinely startled. It was much too soon for Ennis to be returning. Who could it be? He had heard no one approaching and he should have, for in the silence of the evening woods a single footstep would have sounded with the shattering impact of an exploding bomb.

Shrugging off his puzzlement, he went to the front door and opened it a bare crack, peering out.

He recognized the man instantly: John Durgas.

"What do you want here?" Tommy said calmly.

"I thought we might talk."

"No. I don't think we have anything to say."

Durgas smiled. "Why not let me come in and then see?"

"You're not being followed?" he asked.

"I shook off the last of their men years ago. Let me in."

Still, Tommy hesitated. Then he said, "All right. You may as well come in." Carefully they went together into the living room. Tommy sat in the rocking chair and waved Durgas to the couch.

"I prefer to stand," said Durgas.

"Yes. I remember. You always did."

"I haven't changed."

"Yes, I see." His face was as thin and ghostly pale as ever. He wore a dark, neatly pressed business suit and black, well-polished shoes. Large bones protruded through the flesh of his cheeks; a dark stubble decorated his jaw and chin. He had grown a moustache, a slender inverted V. Tommy could read no expression in his eyes.

"What do you want here?" he asked.

"A simple exchange of information," said Durgas.

"I won't tell you a thing."

"That's not what I mean. I'm afraid you misunderstand. I happen to know everything already."

"Then what's the point of this?" Tommy asked.

"The point is that I am the one who is going to exchange the information. I have it; you will hear it. That simple. In return, I will derive a certain degree of pleasure from watching your face as you hear what I have to say. Unless, that is, you'd prefer that I left. If you wish, tell me now. I will go willingly."

"Stay," Tommy said.

Durgas said, "Thank you," but nothing more.

"Do you know," Tommy said suddenly, interrupting his own thoughts, "that I almost killed you one time? I don't mean there at the end. I mean in 1938. I had all the necessary papers prepared. All I had to do was sign my name. And do you know why?"

Durgas nodded carefully.

Tommy ignored the gesture. "It was because I was afraid of you, the same way I'm afraid right now. That was right after you'd purged the Supreme Committee for me. Most of the time I ignored what you accomplished in my name; I assumed you knew what had to be done and was glad to look the other way. But this time. No. I just couldn't believe it. I read the list of the names of the men you had chosen to condemn. Half of them were friends of mine, good friends, real friends, men I had known and trusted since the early twenties. I knew you had to be mad. I wanted you dead. I was determined then to stop you at any cost."

"So why didn't you do it?" Durgas said. "Have me killed?" The impression he gave was that he already knew these answers.

"You know why," Tommy said. "Because I would never have survived without you. How would I know who to trust and who to condemn without you standing at my side and whispering into my ear? I couldn't do it alone. I had to have one man like you. Of all my men, I knew you were the only one who could never be swayed by considerations of friendship or personal loyalty or human devotion. You were one of a kind, Durgas. A really invaluable man."

"I imagine I ought to be grateful for the compliment," Durgas said.

"That won't be necessary. Besides, you know as well as I that it wouldn't have worked. I couldn't have killed you. Lowrey hasn't been able to do it."

"True," Durgas said, "but we're letting the subject slip. My information?"

"All right," Tommy said. "So tell me whatever it is you came here to say."

"You're going to die," Durgas said.

"I know that."

"Do you know when?"

"Why? Did you come here to kill me?"

Durgas laughed pleasantly. "There's no need for that. I came here, as I stated, strictly to exchange some information. Here it is: in one year, exactly one year from today, you will die."

"How do you know?" Tommy said slowly.

"Because that is when you died the last time. July 4, 1947, wasn't it? And today is July 4, 1946."

"You know," Tommy said. He was shaking. "Who told you?"

"Nobody had to tell me."

"What does that mean?"

"It means that I am one too." The smile upon Durgas' lips seemed to spread until it was actually glowing. "The same as you, Tommy."

"No."

"Yes." Durgas waved a languid hand. "I know it all. How you died. The first time. Why. When you were born and reborn."

There was silence. In his own mind Tommy struggled to refute what Durgas had said. Instead, his overwhelming reaction was the opposite to what he desired: he believed him. He would have given his soul to feel otherwise. But nothing else made sense.

"Why are you telling me this?" he asked.

"Why, Tommy," Durgas said, "do you mean to say you don't want to know?" He laughed mockingly. "I thought all lonely men desired some form of company."

"How did it happen?" Tommy spoke eagerly, trying to pretend that Durgas was not who he was. "Was it the same? Did you come from the future like I did?"

Durgas waved once more. "Neither of us came from the future. Not you, not me. This world is the future and that other world; it has its own future, which is not this one. Two separate worlds, Tommy. All things, you see, are possible. And all times. That world where you died, it is a real and substantial place, the same as this. Both exist; they are parallel, if you will, and equal. You appear to believe you have changed the future. Tommy, that is a joke, for you have done no such thing. Look: this is not the same world. It wasn't the same in 1923. John Nance Garner—why wasn't he elected in 1932? Did you cause that change? You were living in San Francisco. Did you ever glance at the morning paper published there?"

"You mean William Randolph Hearst."

"That is correct. In this world, if you care to check, Hearst died as a boy of nine."

"But how does that matter? Garner or Baker? What difference could that possibly make. I was the difference; I made the revolution."

"Of course. I do not deny that. This world is one in which a man named Bloome emerged in the middle nineteen-thirties and effected a revolution of the left in the United States. But that other world, the one from which you came, in that world Bloome never happened. And that fact has not been altered by your activities. That world remains unchanged. And there are other worlds too. Infinitely more others."

Tommy shook his head, unwilling to believe. He had been born again; he had changed history. Any other idea was a lie.

"Even here," Durgas said, "I think you would have failed. Without me, that is. I was the catalyst who allowed your revolution to succeed. Otherwise, you would have failed that first month. You never saw me before I came into your

camp that day. But I knew you, Tommy. I had been waiting."

"This is ridiculous," Tommy said.

"Oh, is it?" Durgas laughed.

Tommy lost his patience, rose from his chair. "Get out of
here!" All at once, he wanted nothing except to ram his
fists through Durgas' grinning face. "I don't have to listen
to you."

"I'm only speaking the truth."

"No!" This time Tommy rejected the concept entirely.
"There's an old Indian down in the settlement. I told him—
he must have told you. The rest of this . . . get out!"

"If you want." Durgas went toward the door.

Tommy grabbed his arm. He turned the man until their
eyes met. He said, "Who are you?"

"Don't you recognize me?"

Tommy held Durgas by the collar, trying to force him to
speak the truth. Durgas' face colored, shifting from red to
blue to violet. He had stopped smiling.

"Tell me," Tommy said. "How do you know? Who told
you?" He spoke evenly, sure of himself. "Who are you? Tell
me or I'll kill you."

Durgas struggled, trying to speak. For a moment Tommy
tightened his grip. Durgas gagged. Then slowly, by degrees,
Tommy let his hands relax. He threw Durgas down. He hit
on his rear; his head whipped back, striking the floor a
solid crack. A pool of blood formed around his head.

Tommy picked him up and shook him easily. He slapped
his face. Durgas flinched back. Tommy let go. Durgas
looked down at the blood on the floor.

"Give me a handkerchief," he said. "Or a towel. I'm bleeding."

"Get out of here."

"Do you want me to bleed to death?"

"You won't."

Durgas said, "I swear I'll kill you," but there was no
force behind his words. The threat was hollow. He went
toward the door. Tommy let him.

At the door, when it was open, Durgas turned back.
"You've got a year. There's nothing you can do to stop it.

I'll be alive to see you die. I know who I am and why. And you, Tommy"—he laughed—"you don't."

He went out the door.

Tommy went to the window and thrust his head outside. He took long, heaving gasps of fresh air; he flooded his lungs.

Then he heard a footstep. Pine needles crackled.

"Who is it?" he cried.

"Me," said a voice. "Only me."

"Oh." Tommy went back to the rocking chair, sat down, picked up the book. A moment later, Ennis entered the cabin. He said nothing, not even about the blood on the floor. Tommy kept silent too. Later that night, he wiped the stain away.

In the morning, he asked Ennis about Tyee John.

"It's funny," Ennis said. "I couldn't find him. Jenny said nobody had seen him since morning. Yesterday morning now. She was afraid he might have gotten in trouble on the water but his boat wasn't gone."

"I'm sure he'll be all right," Tommy said.

"Oh, sure. I imagine he'll show up today. I bet you'll see him today."

Chapter Fifteen

When Tommy Bloome began to die, the fact of his sudden end came as no great surprise to him. He was not eager for death; he was barely even prepared, but knowing in advance that it was coming—and when—and knowing further there was nothing he could do to halt or sway its inexorable approach, made it much easier for him to accept its certain finality. So, a few minutes after eleven o'clock, July 3, 1947, Tommy laid down the book he was reading, rubbed his forehead, and said, "I think I'm getting a headache."

"What is it?" Ennis asked from the couch. "The heat?"

"Yes. It must be the heat. I think I'm going to go lie down for a minute."

"You don't think it's anything serious?"

"Oh, no. Of course not."

Getting to his feet, Tommy tried to move away but, for some mysterious reason, his shoes seemed glued to the floor.

Ennis rushed forward, clutching Tommy by the arm. "What's wrong?" he asked.

"No. I'm all right. Here—here, help me to my room."

When he reached the room, Tommy lay on the bed and asked, his voice already much weaker, if Ennis would mind going away. "I just want to rest for a minute or two. I know it's just the heat." He closed his eyes.

Ennis said, "I'll look in on you later."

"Yes. But I may fall asleep. I'm awfully tired."

"You shouldn't have gone out today."

"I wanted to bag that deer."

"But you missed."

"Yes, I did. Shouldn't have, though." He opened his eyes for a moment. "Close the door on your way out."

"Sure."

He kept his eyes open, straining with the effort, until

Ennis was gone, and then, lowering the lids, he heaved a great sigh. He had much to think about, he realized, but he had not wanted to begin until he was safely alone. Thinking, remembering, these were necessarily private acts. He smiled to himself. The difficult part would now be finding the proper place to begin. He gave a sharp inward laugh. There was no clear beginning. That was the problem. There was an end—yes, to be sure—that lay only a few brief hours into the future—an end, yes, but no beginning.

So he chose to start somewhere in the middle, selecting a moment almost at random. A farm in central California. No, a ranch. He saw a campfire glittering. The flames penetrated deeply, illuminating the dark, hidden places.

An hour later, long before he reached the end of his quest of remembrance, he lost consciousness.

Shortly before one o'clock, looking in upon Tommy once more before retiring, Ennis realized that Tommy was not, as he had thought, asleep. No. The regular rhythmic pattern of his nighttime breathing was clearly absent; in fact, he could not hear Tommy breathing at all. For a moment Ennis was fearful. Tommy couldn't be dead. He was too young; there hadn't been any warning. He rushed desperately into the room and took Tommy's wrist in his hand.

No. He wasn't dead. A strong steady pulse beat here in the wrist. But he was unconscious. His forehead was burning with fever. Ennis went into the bathroom and returned with a cool moist cloth. For the next hour he used this cloth to wipe Tommy's face, but the fever did not lessen. Once or twice during this time Ennis attempted to wake Tommy. On one occasion he thought for certain Tommy had ceased breathing and he searched and searched, willing to accept the faintest pulse as a sign of life, discovering it only after he had nearly surrendered all further hope. It was there. And throbbing as explosively and powerfully as ever. Tommy was alive. For a short time after this, Ennis almost succeeded in convincing himself there was no real danger.

But as the night ran its inexorable course toward dawn, Tommy's pulse began to weaken. His breathing grew louder and fiercer, then shorter and more labored, and the fever burned and burned. Ennis thought about calling someone. Lowrey in Washington. Rachel in California. A doctor? Only the day before Tommy had told him he never wanted a doctor called if he fell sick. Ennis was used to following Tommy's stated desires. He did not act.

In the meantime, shortly before three o'clock Tommy Bloome, fully locked within his own unconscious mind, began to suffer a series of visions. These were more than dreams, having the substance and certainty of life, and were to continue uninterrupted through the night and well into the morning of the following day.

Here is how these visions were:

He is free of his body. A spirit, he soars without physical hindrance. He laughs, exulting in this sudden and unexpected freedom. He swoops through the air, turns somersaults, dives until the earth lies only inches from his face, then rises once more. He cries, shouts, howls with the glorious wonder of true freedom.

A calendar floats past, bearing a single date. Casually it drifts away but, using his hands like a swimmer, he pursues. Catching up, he is able to read the date—with wonder and amazement. The date is today: July 4, 1947. He smiles. Of course. His death day. What other date could it be?

Then he is no longer a part of the sky. Hard, solid wood lies beneath his knees. The platform. He lifts his gaze. The barrel of the gun is a black pit. He barely comprehends the figure of General Norton. From the center of the pit a scarlet flame arises. The bullet hangs suspended within the flames. An explosion rocks the floor under his knees. The bullet spins forward. He wonders, Is this the end come once more?

Then he remembers: but I am a free man. This body cannot contain me. I need not await the arrival of the bullet. And so, laughing, he departs, moving freely, roaming once more.

A whole world lies below him. He is determined to explore it fully. He senses that this world is a familiar place. Why, yes. He grins happily. The world is his own. There is Ennis sitting beside a bed. A man is lying on the bed. Peeking, he sees without surprise that the man is himself. The face is red, beaded with a sprinkling of moisture. Have I been crying? he wonders. But, no, he recollects now, I am merely dying. The thought of death depresses him. Wherever

I go, he thinks, I find myself dying. He attempts to speak with Ennis, and though the words sound clearly and he hears them perfectly well, Ennis fails to respond. Angered, he beats upon Ennis with fists as heavy as steel, drawing blood, suddenly smashing the soft bone of the skull. Still, Ennis does not respond. He continues to wipe the fevered brow of the man on the bed.

Ashamed at what he has done, he flies away, soaring past a squadron of graceful doves. He spies a newspaper spinning past and glimpses a story of himself risking his life in the steaming jungles of East Africa. He pauses to recollect his own youth. The paper falls to earth and is caught by a plain man, who spreads it in his lap and begins to read. Stopping, he drifts down and glances into the man's mind. He must love me, he thinks. All of them do. My people. Murderer, he hears. "No," he cries, "not that, not me." Murderer, thinks the man, reading on. When will you be satisfied? Must every man on Earth die first? Not before then? May God damn your soul down into hell. Murderer. No! No! Again, his fists fall. With neither pity nor regret he pounds the plain man into dust. He laughs at what he has accomplished. Yet the thought remains: murderer.

He glides past Washington, seeing the Tower from where he once ruled. Within the top apartment Lowrey sits, playing poker with a tableful of drunken friends. Lowrey holds the winning hand, but his mind is fogged with drink. Glancing deeper, he seeks his own reflection, but finds only contempt raging like a great fire. And disgust. He hurries away, soaring again. How does Lowrey dare? Without me, you would have been nothing, he thinks. You dare to condemn me.

Now Washington lies far behind. Well, here is Rachel. She sleeps the peaceful, dreamless sleep of a child. A beautiful home surrounds her. And she owes it all to me, he thinks. For a moment he hesitates, fearful of opening old wounds, but since he is dying, he feels no risk can be too great to dare. So he plunges forward, peers inside her sleeping mind, and—

No! The hate, more intense than any fire, drives him out, pursues him as he soars. He screams, "No!" as he sees himself dead, his body brutally severed, torn, splintered. "Not me! Not me! But I love you!"

And the platform lies once more beneath his knees. His body accepts the return of its spirit. The bullet edges closer. He sees clearly the narrow creases upon its whirling tip; he hears the whistle of air rushing behind. He screams, afraid this time that it will reach him. And—

Another world. Soaring free again, he plunges. Children cluster in a circle. A band blares forth a ringing patriotic anthem. Upon a raised platform a man addresses the crowd, waving his arms furiously, shouting such words as "America," "independence," "liberty," and "freedom." But he does not listen, for he is more concerned with the roaring exploding candle that sends a circle of children vaulting away in a laughing, chaotic, shouting mass. A banner flies open. HAPPY FOURTH OF JULY. He, too, is happy. This day is his day as well.

He peeks into one of the minds within the crowd. Why, there is nothing. The man does not know him. Then who is his leader? What world is this? He glimpses a vague portrait of a plain man with rimless spectacles and a brisk, quick way of talking and moving. He does not know this man. Rising again, gliding gently now, he gazes down upon the naked fertile land below. The world he sees is well-fed, prosperous, outwardly content, but beneath this exterior of tranquillity lies a deeper, more painful core of fear. He understands at last that this is a world in which the old system has survived and grown stronger. How? He wishes to learn more. But—too late. Beneath him the bomb explodes. The city dies beneath a great, gathering cloud. The air itself is on fire. The flames chase him across the sky. A shock wave washes over him, tossing him back toward the inferno behind. His lips part. He tries to scream and—

Again, the platform. The bullet. It edges narrowly close now. But he is prepared this time. He stays only a microsecond, then rises, soars, seeing his body behind as a—

The world is green. A vast forest reaches across the whole of the continent. In the few places where the forest does not grow, a wide plain extends briefly. Great herds of bison wander peaceably. He is confused. How can this be 1947? Ahead, abruptly, he spies a man crawling toward the herd.

A naked man. A red man. Inside this man's mind, he finds nothing to alleviate his puzzlement. Superstitions dominate facts. And hunger. From kindness, he uses his powers to slay a nearby buffalo. The animal topples like a felled tree. The Indian rushes forward, shouting his gratitude to invisible gods in nature. Laughing, he soars across the eastern ocean and reaches the old continent. Here he finds men like himself. Fields are plowed by hand. A dead horse lies rotting in the center of the town square. Church bells chime loudly. Names are sought but not discovered: Marx, Napoleon, Hitler, Bloome, Stalin, Lincoln, Darwin. This is a static world. Even the wind barely moves. A procession passes. Men naked to their waists. They move carefully, beating savagely upon their own bared backs with whips made from wood and leather. Christ is praised, glorified, proclaimed Son of Man. He flees.

The platform. The spinning bullet. The weight of his own body. Flesh and blood and bone and muscle. Closer, ever closer. If he wished, he could touch the tip now.

But there is no time for rest.

This world is different again. He fails to recognize where he is at first, for the absence of cities leads him to expect a world similar to the last, but eventually he understands that this is not so. In fact, the continent is fully occupied. Many villages lie speckled here and there between the two great oceans He draws close to one. The inhabitants are not Indians; they are a racially mixed people: part red, white, some black. He observes these people working long hours in the fields that surround their village. Within their minds, he glimpses a great sense of contentment. One name rises above all others: the name is his own. To these people, he is a savior, though not a leader. They love but do not worship him. At dusk they leave the fields and repair to their make-shift huts and listen to the radio. A bulletin is read concerning a certain unexpected death. The whole world weeps. But how can this be? The world is not his. Why should they know him here? Within his confusion lies a growing fear. Before this fear can expand to consume him, he rises, soaring above this peaceful world. Below, children stop and wave to him. Then he remembers his name. What he has feared comes true. My name, he thinks. The one they worship is

Tommy Bloome, yes, but my name is Timothy O'Mara. I killed Bloome. Murdered him. He is dead.

And the platform. The gun. Bullet whistling in the air. He pauses this time long enough to peer beyond the bullet. The sky seems open to him. He lies at the center, the hub of a vast wheel, the spokes of which stretch endlessly away in infinite number. Each spoke, he realizes, is a pathway to another world. How can he possibly choose? The bullet draws inexorably closer, closer. He selects a path in desperation, vaults forward, rushes down its length.

Below him lies the new world and immediately he knows he has chosen poorly. The green, blue lushness of the cloud wreathed Earth is gone. Below lies a round ball of dead ash. He pleads for the presence of life but is granted nothing. He circles the planet again and again; it is a dead world. When? What? How? Why? He senses the absence of pure air and is grateful he need not breathe. He refuses to mourn the death of this world. Given an infinite number of alternatives, such a world must be inevitable. But he is not glad he has gazed upon it. This vision will haunt his consciousness forever.

Without hesitation, he turns and rushes down the pathway. Ahead, in the hub, he sees his physical form awaiting death. He tries to turn away. But having come this far, he cannot change direction; inertia draws him straight to the center. Again, he enters his own body. He feels the bullet. Its glowing tip touches his forehead. He screams, dives, vaults. A new pathway opens ahead.

A new world.

He sees himself in his physical form, standing upon a platform. Before him a crowd stretches away, thousands upon thousands. Men. Women. Children too. Drawing closer, he lands among these people and senses their love reaching out to embrace the man upon the platform above. Looking around, he surveys the faces surrounding him. Why, here is Lowrey standing right beside him and he senses the immense gratitude Lowrey has for all that has been done for him. And Rachel—proud woman—here she is, beaming with joy, glowing with love. At her side stands her father, and he is thinking what a truly great man this is, what grand things he has accomplished to benefit all mankind. And more. Here is Bob Ennis—true friend. And a girl—Nadine—she loves him deeply. The victims from the wall are here, alive, worshiping together. Everyone, together, in unison, they scream, Tommy, Tommy, Tommy. He screams with them, unwilling to restrain himself, Tommy, Tommy, Tommy.

How did I do it? he wonders. Why do they love me here and hate me there? What is this world? What am I? Who? The entire crowd is weeping joyously now, their tears threatening to consume a whole world.

He springs forward in an attempt to confront himself. He must ask this man why. And how. Running swiftly. Bounding up the steps to the platform. Beneath his feet the wood echoes solidly. He sees himself turn.

He shouts, "Help me! I want to know! Please tell me!"

But this man cannot help him. He staggers back.

The face is not his own: it is John Durgas.

He is gone. The world bursts and it is gone. The man with the gun stands before him. The platform under his knees. The bullet effortlessly penetrates his skull. Wait, wait, he tries to scream. Not yet, please not yet, not yet . . .

He sees past the gun. A face beyond the edge of his vision. Durgas. Again. Here. Watching.

No!

Then his head explodes. His eyes shatter with the pain. His body rises, falls, rises once more.

The wheel is gone. There is nothing now—no escape. For the last time he screams, "No!"

And then, after this, there is nothing. Absolutely nothing.